Jean Paul, traveler

LADY GREEN SATIN

AND

HER MAID ROSETTE

THE HISTORY OF JEAN PAUL
AND HIS LITTLE WHITE MICE

TRANSLATED FROM THE FRENCH OF THE
BARONESS E. MARTINEAU DES CHESNEZ

With an Introduction by
CLARA WHITEHILL HUNT

And Illustrations by
WINIFRED BROMHALL

WILDSIDE PRESS

CONTENTS

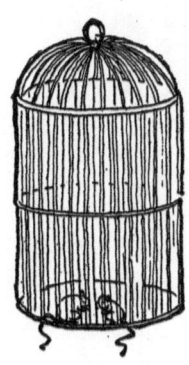

ILLUSTRATIONS

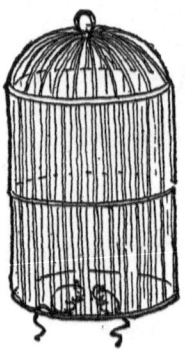

INTRODUCTION

IT is the opinion of our most far-seeing leaders that one of the chief causes of war is the ignorance of the great mass of people regarding those who speak a different language and live under a different government from their own. This ignorance breeds narrow-mindedness, prejudice, provincialism of outlook, from which a few bad leaders can easily manage to create misunderstandings which inevitably are followed by a resort to arms.

It is no wonder that the best statesmen urge the training of our citizens in the habit of the "international mind," for only as every least voter comes to have breadth of outlook and sympathy for people of other lands can we hope to do away with that trait of the barbarian who survives in every ignorant human, prejudice against anyone whose ways and speech are unlike his own.

A very solemn and quite irrelevant introduction to a simple story of a little French peasant boy, this may seem. Those, however, who are best acquainted with young children and who have studied the effect of early prejudices upon the whole life, know that one of the surest means of arousing an interest which will survive the passage of years is to give to children stories that will take strong hold upon their imaginations. Many an adult who has never seen Switzerland loves that beautiful land for the sake of "Heidi," whose story was first heard from mother's lips at bedtime reading hour.

There are a number of lovely stories of other lands to which all children should have access, but the number is small. The written-to-order, supplementary-reading-book affair is not the sort that contributes what we mean. It is the story by a writer who understands and loves children, who possesses imagination and style, who has an intimate personal knowledge of his subject and an eagerness to make his characters live in the hearts of his young readers that will make a lasting and a valuable impression.

Years ago a much worn volume containing the story of Jean Paul and his performing mice was called to my attention by an adult who told me that this little book had had exactly the effect upon her which I have described. Her interest in the country of Jean Paul and Madeleine, made real to her by the story of these beloved children, did not cease with childhood but grew with her growth.

While this is a tale of another generation, its appeal

to the unspoiled child reader of today will be the greater because of its quaint differentness from the child's own life; and those American children who have "adopted" French war orphans will have an especially warm interest in the fatherless boy who so bravely helped his mother and sisters.

If this little book becomes a means of wakening in even a few of our boys and girls a love for the gallant land of Lafayette it will have justified the faith which has led to its reprinting.

CLARA WHITEHILL HUNT.

Brooklyn, April, 1923.

LADY GREEN SATIN

AND

HER MAID ROSETTE

Chapter I

Showing what an errand well done brought to Jean Paul

DO you see the little boy climbing that steep hill? He is on his way to Escaladios, a little village in the Pyrenees. What a large pitcher he is carrying! How heavy it must be! It is so full—he is carrying it very steadily, fearing to spill a drop of the pure water which he has gone so far to seek.

I will tell you his name: it is Jean Paul, and his mother's name is Jane. He lives yonder, on the hill, in that poor cottage. Every day in good or bad weather he goes to the spring at the end of the village to fill his big pitcher and to mount with it along the great highway. Sometimes the sun is burning, sometimes the snow chills his little feet, or the rain wets him to the skin—Jean Paul never fails to go. He has also other tasks: he picks up the deadwood in the forest, he gleans the fields after harvest, and he gathers grass to feed his rabbits.

Jean Paul is about nine years old and he is not large for his age. But he knows that he must work with all his strength. His father is dead; and his mother is very weak and sad since the death of this beloved father, and his four little sisters are all younger than he. The youngest, the little Marie, does not walk yet, so when Jean Paul returns to the house he takes her in his arms and walks with her in the road; it is he who lulls her to sleep, and who puts her to bed. Jean Paul has so much resolution and good will that one might say that he knew how to do everything.

One day when he had been holding Marie in his arms before their cottage, he entered quickly, and gave the child to his mother Jane. "Have the goodness to take her, mother," said he. "Monsieur Legras is calling me; without doubt he has an errand for me to do, and this evening I will bring you back a nice ten-sous piece." While speaking, he embraced his mother, put on his little cap, and ran to meet a big farmer who was on the road beckoning to him. The farmer took a letter from his pocket and explained to the child that he must carry it to its address without loss of time, and bring back an answer. "You have two leagues to go, and two leagues to come back, my little man," said M. Legras, "but it is yet early, and you will be able to return home to your mother before night. The person to whom you carry this letter will give you your dinner." Jean Paul set off quickly; he knew the road well, for he had gone over almost the whole of it before.

Three o'clock was striking when he knocked at a large door, and asked for M. Thibault. "I have a letter for him which requires an immediate answer." M. Thibault was out. His servant made the little messenger come in, and gave him something to eat and drink. Soon after he fell asleep upon a chair waiting the return of the master of the house. Suddenly some one woke him up and handed him a letter. "Go quickly, my child; here is the answer which you have asked for. Carry it without delay to M. Legras. Take these ten sous to pay for your trouble, and this piece of bread and glass of cider." Jean Paul rubbed his eyes, drank the glass of cider, which woke him up completely, put the bread in his cap, and the ten-sous piece in the corner of his handkerchief, which he tied up carefully, made a bow, and set off gaily, the letter in his hand.

Jean Paul did not suspect that he had been asleep three long hours. At the moment he started six o'clock struck; in an hour it would be dark. Jean Paul did not see a great black cloud which advanced so quickly that it would soon cover the sky entirely. The child sang as he walked, and looked to the right and left, thinking at the same time of his dear mother and his little sisters. "The ten-sous piece shall be for my mother, but this big piece of white bread shall be for my sisters, who will like it much better than the black bread they eat every day. Happy day!" said the good little Jean Paul, jumping with joy.

Suddenly he felt large and heavy drops of rain fall on his face and hands, a severe flash of lightning dazzled him, the thunder seemed to burst above his head, while the rain increased, and night had come on. Happily the child had but a short distance to go before arriving at one of those stables where cattle are kept during the winter. He ran quickly thither, shut the door, shook the water from his clothes, reflected a moment, then knelt down to thank God for all the good things He had given to him during the past day, and prayed that He would protect him during the coming night.

And now behold him lying on the ground with a bundle of hay under his head, sleeping tranquilly, while the rain is pouring down, and the thunder shakes the earth and the lightning seems to tear the heavens. Jean Paul sleeps as quietly as if he were sleeping by the side of his mother. Why should he be afraid of the storm? Does he not know that it is God who causes the storm as well as the sunshine? Does he not know that the good God watches over him the same as if it were a bright moonlight night? And then Jean Paul has that peace in his heart which God has promised to give to the good.

Near midnight Jean Paul awoke. The thunder had ceased, but the rain fell in torrents, and the child heard it falling on the roof of the stable. He had already slept several hours in the daytime and was no longer sleepy; he seated himself upon his pillow of hay, and began to look around him without seeing anything at all, as it was a dark night. After a little while he felt hungry, as all children do when they awake. He thought of his piece of white bread, but all at once he thought also of his little sisters. "Bah!" said he to himself. "I can wait very well until breakfast time tomorrow morning when I shall be at home."

"He, he! he, he, he! he, he!" Jean Paul did not move; he held his breath; he saw something like great red beads which shone through the darkness, and he heard again, but more distinctly, *"He! he! he!"* This time the bright beads had changed their places and had come quite near him. Jean Paul leaned forward to catch them. He caught in each hand something warm and soft. The moon at this moment shone through the clouds, and Jean Paul saw with delight that he had in each hand a little mouse as white as snow. It was their eyes that he had seen shining in the darkness. Now he could see their little red feet, their tiny ears, their pretty, long, slender tails.

At the moment Jean Paul had caught them, the little rogues were creeping into his cap, which he had placed by his side, and were beginning to nibble the nice bread which he had put there for his sisters. They had been there a long time during his sleep, for they had nibbled it in more than one place. In spite of this, Jean cannot call these pretty animals enough pet names. He cannot caress them, for his two hands are busy holding them, and if he releases his hold ever so little he feels that the nimble little creatures will run away. In the meantime he ceases to hear the rain fall on the roof; the wind is lulled, the moon is so bright one might think it was

day. Jean Paul said to himself that it was time to start
for home. But where should he put the dear little
animals? After reflecting well, he slipped them one
after the other into his blouse, and as soon as his hands
were free, tightened his belt around his waist, in order
that they might not escape; then he put on his cap and
started on his way. But the rogues! what races they
ran in the poor, worn-out blouse! how they tickled Jean
Paul! Ha! here they are in his sleeves; one of them
even runs up his back. They begin to gnaw the cloth,
which is so old that their little teeth tear it easily.
Luckily Jean Paul put his hand over the hole at the
moment a little white head peeped out of it and seized
the runaway. An idea strikes him! He puts the little
fellow in his cap, which he holds firmly on his head,
and with the hand that is free, he takes the other mouse
from his blouse, puts it also in his cap, takes his handkerchief from his pocket, passes it over his head and
ties it firmly under his chin, after assuring himself that
the dear ten sous piece was safe. His cap is made of
very strong leather, and Jean Paul's hair is so thick,
that he neither feels the little feet that run, nor the little
teeth which try to bite.

"Halloo, mice!" said he to them on starting again,
"you are in a nice little granary; you will not die there
of hunger, for you have that piece of white bread that
you have already begun to eat, little thieves! I will let
you finish it; do you hear?" Jean Paul laughed heartily, jumped with joy, and started off running.

It was a very fine night after the storm. It was so
calm, nature seemed to be asleep; nothing was heard
but the water of the swollen streams which ran along

the highway, and now and then, *"He! he! he!"* in Jean Paul's cap. "Be good, up there!" said he, and he gave a little knock on his head.

The moon still shone when Jean Paul entered his mother's house. He passed by his sleeping sisters without making a noise. Instead of going to bed, he climbed lightly a little ladder which was placed in the corner of the chamber, and which led to a miserable garret. There was a great trunk there, where mother Jane formerly locked up the linen and clothes of the family, but now the poor woman and her children had no other clothes than those they wore every day, and the trunk was empty. Jean Paul opened it partly and slipped into it the two little mice, one after the other. He then crumbled the bread which was left in his cap, and threw it into the trunk which he shut without making a noise; then he descended the ladder quietly, went to bed, and slept.

He was not the last one to get up the next morning. As soon as he opened his eyes, he remembered the letter that M. Thibault had given him, dressed himself quietly, and ran with it to M. Legras. The good man insisted upon giving him another ten-sous piece. In vain Jean Paul told him that he had been paid by M. Thibault. "It is on account of the storm that I give it," said M. Legras.

Jean Paul returned home quite proud. "Look what I have brought you!" said he, embracing his mother, and giving her the two pieces of money. "And I have brought for my sisters—" here he stopped suddenly. He was going to say, "two little white mice," but he thought that his sisters would all go up together to the garret to see the little creatures, they would open the trunk, and would let them run away—he stopped then.

"What—what have you brought us?" said the little girls.

"Plenty of kisses," said Jean Paul, and he embraced them all, one after the other.

"Well, then, it is we who are going to surprise you!" cried the little girls. "You shall see!" The three eldest surrounded Jean Paul, and left little Marie at the other end of the room. "Hold out your arms to her, Jean Paul. Marie walked all alone, yesterday, after you went away," cried the elder ones. "Marie, come; little Marie come!"

The dear little one came forward to her brother, and he caught her in his arms. "Bravo, Marie! Bravo!" said all the children, and they covered her with kisses.

Chapter II

Our two Heroines are presented to the reader

A MONTH afterward the mother, Jane, was sewing, seated on a bench at the door of her house.
Her little daughters were running and playing near
her. She looked about for Jean Paul and did not see
him.

"Go and look for him!" said she. "I am sure that
he is in the garret. What can he be doing there?
Jean Paul is very much changed; formerly, unless some
work obliged him to go out, he was always with his
sisters, or by me; now, as soon as he has brought the
water in the morning, he goes up into that miserable
garret and remains there until he comes to eat his soup.
It is true that Marie walks now and she does not require
him so much.

"But what can he be doing there all alone? When I

go up unexpectedly I always find him sitting upon the big trunk, looking uneasy. If I ask him why he stays there, he replies that he is amusing himself. He is a good boy, Jean Paul, and he used to be a good worker."

While his mother is asking herself these questions, let us go and see what our friend Jean Paul is doing in his garret. Here he is, climbing up the last step of the ladder and entering on tiptoe. He puts his hand in his pocket, from which he takes a crust of cheese and some crumbs of bread, the remains of his breakfast. Then he raises the lid of the big trunk and presents to the two mice his hand filled with bread and cheese, like a little dinner table. He begins to laugh when he sees these two little creatures seating themselves by his hand, taking up the pieces with their fore paws and putting them in their mouths. The meal being over, Jean Paul makes them jump over a little stick, which he holds each time a little higher, that they may learn to jump very high; and then he orders them to wash themselves, and the two little creatures rub their noses with their small feet. "Now, you, who are the biggest, pretend to be sick, and the little one must take care of madame." Then one of the mice laid itself down in the corner of the big trunk, whilst the other went backwards and forwards, coming near to its companion and putting its little feet over its body. "Very good!" said Jean Paul, "I am satisfied with you; you improve."

He was going to shut up the trunk, when ever so many little hands held up the cover. "More, more!" said little Marie, who wanted the little creatures to repeat their tricks. The three other little girls cried also with all their might, "Again! again!" Jean Paul

THE LITTLE GIRLS CRIED WITH ALL THEIR MIGHT, "AGAIN, AGAIN!"

11

was surprised and frightened at being surrounded in this manner. He had been so deeply interested in his pupils that he had not heard his sisters come up. The mice were still more surprised and frightened than he: one of them, seeing the trunk wider open than usual, took advantage of it to climb to the top, and jumping lightly on the floor, he ran away so very quickly that they could not see where he was. The little girls pursued him everywhere, screaming and laughing. Poor Jean Paul was in despair: "Mother! mother!" cried he, "have pity on me! and call to my sisters to come down. Come, mother, come, and take them away, I beg of you; they prevent me from catching my mouse! Mother, come, help me!" His mother did not understand very well what misfortune had happened to Jean Paul nor what he was looking for; but the cries of the poor boy were so beseeching that she ran quickly up into the garret, took little Marie into her arms, and made the other three children go down before her. "Mother," said Jean Paul in a whisper, "have the goodness to go down also with Marie, and I will tell you all in a moment." Jean Paul looked so unhappy that his good mother complied with his request and took away with her little Marie, who kept calling out, "The little mice, more, more!"

When Jean Paul was alone and all was quiet in the garret, he remained motionless, holding his breath that he might make less noise. But his eyes were not still, they looked everywhere. At last he saw appear between two old pieces of wood the point of a little white nose. He at first thought of running forward to catch it, but he said to himself, "It would not be a good plan, as it

can run much faster than I." Then he felt in his pocket
for some crumbs of bread, and began to call to it as
he did every day when he opened the trunk, "Mini!
little one! come to your master. Mini! Mini!" The
little creature did not move. Jean Paul continued patiently to call it. At last it put its head outside of its
hiding place, first one foot, then the other, came forward a few steps, and finally began to nibble the bread
which Jean Paul held in his hand.

He waited until the mouse was engrossed in eating,
then adroitly caught hold of him, put him in the big
trunk, placed a heavy piece of wood on top of the trunk
and went down to his mother and sisters.

He told them very quickly the whole history of his
two little prisoners; where he had found them, and the
trouble he had in bringing them home in his cap, and
how he had passed many hours with them ever since
they had been in the garret.

He recounted to them how by degrees he had tamed
them, that now they knew and obeyed him and ate
from his hand. "Oh, yes! Oh, yes!" interrupted all the
little girls, "they are so funny, so cunning, mother; let
us go back to the garret! Jean Paul is going to show
them to us and we shall see them again. Come quickly!"
And the little girls pulled their mother to the side of
the ladder which led to the garret.

"Mother, I have not told you all," said Jean Paul.
"Just now, when my sisters were up there, they frightened my little pupils so much that one of them ran away.
I would never have been able to catch it again if you
had not been so kind as to make my sisters go down
stairs and leave me up there alone. I am sure that the

poor creatures are still so frightened that they could do nothing well—I beg you, my dear mother, to wait until to-morrow."

His mother thought that Jean Paul was right. The great performance was to be put off until the next day. The little girls spoke of nothing but, the white mice all the rest of the day, and it was their first thought when they awoke the next morning. "Little mousies!" said Marie, when she first opened her eyes. Jean Paul was already with his pupils, and he remained with them until breakfast time. When the meal was over he took off the tablecloth, wiped the table, placed the chairs all around it, and begged his mother and sisters to sit down, while he shut the door and windows carefully, and went up into his garret. The little girls stamped their feet with joy when they saw him come down with the two little animals. "Take care, Jean Paul; they are going to run away!" they all cried at once. Jean Paul had no fear of that; he had tied a string securely to one of the hind feet of each mouse, and held the end. The string was long enough to let them walk and jump. The performance succeeded admirably; Jean Paul's pupils ate from his hand, jumped over the little stick, and concluded the performance as they did the night before, by pretending to be dead. The little girls were wild with joy and their mother was very much amused.

"One might suppose they were ladies and that they had sense," said little Angéle.

"Yes, but what a pity that they are not dressed like ladies!" answered Louisa.

"Mamma works so nicely, she might make them dresses," Caroline said.

"Oh, yes! dresses for the little mice! and shawls! and little hats!" they all cried at once, throwing their arms around their mother's neck.

"Yes, yes, I should like to make them, my children; I will try, but it will not be easy," answered their mother, freeing herself from all the little arms.

The mice having shown all their accomplishments, Jean Paul took advantage of this tumult to carry them back again into their trunk; but he had hardly come down the ladder when his sisters surrounded him, crying:

"Jean Paul, run quick and bring down the little mice; mamma wants to take their measure; she is going to make dresses for them—hats, shawls, petticoats, everything! Mamma said so!"

His mother nodded yes, in answer to Jean Paul's inquiring look—for as the little girls all spoke at once, it was impossible to understand in any other manner. Jean Paul, delighted, ran lightly up the ladder and came down with his two little animals. Their mother measured their length and breadth with narrow strips of paper.

She measured also the length of their paws and the size of their neck, and so on.

When the mice were put back in their prison the noise ceased by degrees.

The mother then said, "Children, go immediately to your work, if you wish me to keep my promise of making garments for your brother's little pupils this evening. Jean Paul, go and cut some grass for the rabbits, which you have neglected so much lately. Angéle, take your knitting; Louise, sweep the house and put the dishes away; and you two little ones, amuse yourselves, but do not go far away from me." While speaking, their mother began her work. They were not little doll's clothes that she was making—no! she was mending the coarse shirts and chemises of Jean Paul and his sisters.

All the children obeyed their mother; the eldest began working, while the younger seated themselves upon the ground by her side.

In the evening, when they were all in bed and asleep, their mother began to look at the measures she had taken in the morning. "What can I make these little dresses with?" said she to herself. "I have nothing but old faded rags." Suddenly she got up and opened the top drawer in an old sideboard; she just remembered a green satin bow that had been given to her before her marriage, when she had been godmother. The bow was wrapped up in paper and was still quite fresh, and the ribbon was wide. The good mother, consulting the little measures, set to work at cutting the stuff and then sewing it very neatly. Before her marriage she had lived in a city and had been a very good mantua-maker. There! the little petticoat is done, then the little bodice and the little narrow sleeves.

But she is very tired and the light makes her eyes water. "Bah!" said she to herself, "I will have time to make the little hat this evening; there is still a little stuff left. The poor children will be so delighted to-morrow."

In spite of her fatigue, the good mother worked part of the night. When she left her worktable she held in her hand a pretty little dress of green satin, all puffed—

and a darling little hat of the same. stuff as the dress. She locked all these things carefully in the upper drawer of the sideboard and then she went to bed.

How delighted the children were the next day, when their mother, without saying a word, took from the drawer of the sideboard the pretty little clothes! The little girls wanted to try them on the mice immediately, but their mother asked them to wait until the other little dress was made, and Jean Paul thought it was better to do so.

"When they are both dressed we will play a complete comedy, I promise you," said he.

"Yes, but what shall we make the second dress with? I have neither ribbon nor silk," his mother said.

"There is still a little piece left of the pink calico, that my godfather gave.me, that will be pretty enough," said little Alice.

"Especially alongside of this splendid. green satin," answered Louise.

"At any rate," said their mother, who held in her hand the piece of pink calico which she had taken from the drawer, "I have nothing else. This little square of white muslin is so small that it is useless to speak of it; so, if you will not have this calico, my children, the little mouse will have no other dress than the white one that the good God has given to her."

"Oh, mamma!" said Jean Paul, "I beg you to make the pink dress for her; you are so skilful, and besides, it will be very pretty."

The little children whispered to each other, and said the calico was very ugly; that it was a great pity; and often through the day they looked in every place they could think of, hoping to find a piece of pretty silk; but they looked in vain.

As she had done the night before, when the children had gone to bed, the mother began to work; as before, she worked part of the night; and as before, she put her work when it was finished in the drawer of the old sideboard, and went to bed very tired.

Angéle and her sisters were very much astonished on waking the next morning to find themselves alone in their room. Their mother had gone to wash on the banks of the river; but where was Jean Paul? The little children washed and dressed themselves, the biggest helping the little ones; they said their prayers, and each of them took a piece of bread from the sideboard, all laughing and talking of the pretty mousies, as Marie called them. They had not finished their breakfast when their mother came in, and at the same time Jean Paul came down from the garret holding in his hand his two little pupils, which he put on the table.

The largest was dressed in the magnificent dress of green satin, which fitted it extremely well; the petticoat was so long, and nicely puffed out, and when my lady the mouse stood up and walked, the train had a most graceful appearance.

"Oh, how beautiful she is!" said all the children.

"One would say that she was a noble lady, with her long train," said Angéle.

"She looks like a noble lady," replied the little Caroline, although she could not have explained what a noble lady was, but she thought it was a very fine thing.

"But, look," said Louise, "how pretty the other is,

with her short pink dress and her little peasant's cap of muslin!"

"How hard mother has worked!" said Jean Paul, looking affectionately at his mother.

"And look at her pretty white apron!" said Angéle.

"She might pass for the maid of my lady Green Satin," said Louisa.

"My lady Green Satin, that is it! Let us call her my lady Green Satin. And let us call her maid Rosette," said Angéle.

"Yes! yes! yes!" all cried at once, "my lady Green Satin and her maid Rosette."

And all the children clapped their hands while repeating, "My lady Green Satin and her maid Rosette."

"My lady, you are wanted to begin the play, and you, also, Miss Rosette," said the sweet voice of Angéle. "Do not make us wait too long."

"The play! the play!" all the children cried while seating themselves around the table.

Jean Paul very seriously commanded my lady mouse to begin by making a bow. My lady stood on her hind feet, made a very low bow, which Rosette returned very politely.

Both mother and children roared out laughing, for the long, white, slender tail of Rosette was seen below her dress. Marie was taking her little knife from her pocket—"to tut it," she said. Fortunately for Rosette, Jean Paul already had tucked it up and fastened it adroitly under her petticoat.

"Silence!" said he, raising his voice. "Silence!" And everybody looked at little Rosette waiting on my lady Green Satin while she breakfasted.

The obedient Rosette, standing all the time on her hind legs, came running to Jean Paul, and took from his hands a little waiter of paper on which there was a piece of bread and piece of sugar; then, still running, she carried it to her mistress, who with her front feet, took the bread and sugar very daintily and put them in her mouth, while Rosette stood up before her, holding the waiter.

"Oh, how nice they are! how pretty it is!" began the little girls——

"Silence!" said Jean Paul again, with a loud voice.

"My lady has breakfasted and wishes to take a walk. Come, Rosette! put on your mistress's boots, give her her hat, and take care that she does not muddy her new dress."

My lady seated herself upon a little wooden bench that Jean Paul had made expressly for her. Rosette knelt down in front of her. My lady held out her hind feet one after the other, and Rosette pretended to put on her boots. Then Rosette got up and took from Jean Paul's hand the little green hat and presented it to her mistress. Then my lady put it on her head in such a funny manner that the children and their mother burst out laughing again. It was still worse when my lady began slowly and gracefully to walk around the table, while Rosette held up the green satin trail very respectfully.

Then Jean Paul's mother and sisters laughed so violently that the two little frightened animals got down on their four feet, and would have escaped if their clothes had not prevented them from running.

The fear of seeing the performance interrupted and

a loud "Hush, there!" from Jean Paul quieted the laughers.

"Now, my lady, you are tired with your walk—I beg you to lie down. Rosette, help your mistress, and take care of her; I am afraid she is going to be sick." My lady, in the most graceful manner, laid herself down upon the ground. Rosette came near her, arranged the folds of her dress, took hold of her paw, as if she was going to feel her pulse, and stroked her forehead. My lady shut her eyes and let her head fall.

"Rosette," said Jean Paul very sadly and slowly, "you see that your poor mistress is dead. The best thing that you can do is to die, also."

At these words Rosette fell down alongside of her mistress, bent her head and shut her eyes.

The little children had all stood up that they might see better—they scarcely breathed. Little Marie sobbed, as she believed the little creatures were dead. Caroline began to cry also.

"How pale they are!" said she in a whisper to Louise. Their mother wanted to laugh, for certainly the white hair which covered the pointed noses of the mice had not changed color; but she tried to look serious that she might not disconcert her daughters.

Then Jean Paul tapped his hands and began singing a country air, in which, by degrees, all the sisters joined. At the first sound my lady and Rosette jumped up, put their arms around each other, and began to waltz, then to jump very high, and to leap in the funniest manner, crying, *"He! he! He! he!"*

Marie clapped her hands and sang as loud as the others. Sometimes my lady and Rosette danced opposite each other, sometimes they caught each other around the waist and turned wildly.

"Hop!" Jean Paul said all at once, when the little creatures seemed most engaged in dancing; and suddenly they nestled in their master's hands as if they were in a little nest.

Jean Paul's sisters would have said "More," as little Marie had done, but Jean Paul made each one of them put their fingers over the heart of the poor little creatures, and they felt it beat as if it would break. There was now no other amusement for the day excepting to see my lady and her little maid undress—and they seemed very glad to be relieved from their elegant clothes.

Chapter III

*A great step is taken, about which my lady and Rosette
are not consulted*

VERY often during the following week his little
sisters begged Jean Paul to show them again my
lady and Rosette. Jean Paul was never tired of showing them, nor the children of looking at them. The
neighbors, who had had a glimpse of them through the
little window, asked permission to enter that they might
admire them at their ease. By degrees the reputation
of my lady and her maid extended; they were spoken
of not only in Escaladios, but even in the neighboring
village.

But in the meantime the villagers were anxious, and
looked sad. The summer was over; they were busy
reaping the corn, and it was said everywhere that the

harvest was bad, that wheat was scarce, and that bread would be dear, very dear, all the winter. Jean Paul's mother was paler and sadder than usual. She prayed a long time both morning and evening; she asked herself how she would be able to feed all these dear beings who depended upon her. And she prayed to God to aid her. Jean Paul was always very active and hard working, but he could scarcely earn anything; all the dead wood seemed to be gathered before it fell from the trees; there was no more money to be gained by running errands for the farmers, for they would not spend their money; no more ears of corn to glean, the reapers had gathered them so carefully.

Jean Paul tried to show his dear little animals with their pretty costumes in the neighboring villages; but my lady and Rosette displayed all their graces and pretty tricks in vain, and Jean Paul had very rarely any sous to take to his mother, for although the peasants seemed well pleased, they had nothing to give him.

One day when Jean Paul was sitting at the door of their house, looking sadly before him without seeing anything, he heard the cracking of a whip and the noise of wheels. A carriage was coming slowly up the hill; it had already almost reached their house. The coachman had come down from his seat and was walking alongside of his horses. Very few carriages passed this steep road. Jean Paul admired this one very much: it was an elegant open carriage; a young man was seated on the high seat in front; in the carriage was an enormous quantity of pink and white muslin. "Six handsome dresses, at least," said Jean Paul to himself; but he saw the smiling faces of only two young ladies.

"My child," said one of them to him, just as the carriage passed him, "does a woman of the name of Jane live here?"

Jean Paul was so astonished, so wonderstricken, that he did not answer, and the carriage would have gone on if his mother, who was in the house and had heard the question, had not run out to say that this was Jane's house and that she was Jane.

It was not she that these fine ladies wished to see. They had just arrived at a neighboring chateau, where they found it very dull, and having heard their maids speaking of the famous Lady Green Satin and her maid, Rosette, they had made Jane's poor house the object of their drive, and now asked to see the little wonders.

As soon as these fine ladies had pronounced the name of his dear lady Green Satin, Jean Paul understood it all.

While they were telling his mother the object of their visit, he ran up into the garret, dressed the little animals quickly, and came down, carrying them on the back of his hand.

But how was he to show them the performance they wished to see? It was impossible to ask them to come into their poor kitchen and to seat themselves around the table where the mice ordinarily played. There were no chairs fit to hold such magnificent dresses! Jean Paul was for a moment in despair; fortunately he saw in the corner the board on which his mother ironed her clothes. His mother brought it to the carriage; the footman opened the door for Jean Paul, who was holding his little animals still in his hand, and he seated himself on the high front seat by the side of the young man. It seemed to him at first that my lady and Rosette were, so to speak, drowned in the folds of these immense muslin skirts, which spread out on all sides; then he got up resolutely and remained standing. The ironing board was placed firmly on the knees of the young man and sustained by the strong hands of the footman; then the play commenced.

The little animals were more active, more graceful, more intelligent than ever; the ladies laughed a great deal, and declared that my lady and Rosette were "adorable," and that even in Paris they had never seen anything like it.

"Do you know," said one of them to the gentleman, "that at Paris this young fellow would make money by showing these little animals?"

Then all three took out their purses; three pieces fell into the hand of Jean Paul; the ironing board was taken away, the little animals jumped into the arms of their master, the coachman mounted again to his place, the carriage turned around, went down the hill, and was soon out of sight.

"Mother!" cried Jean Paul, "a twenty-sous piece, a forty-sous piece, and a gold ten-sous piece!"

"You had better say a ten-franc piece, little simpleton!" replied his mother. "Poor children!" added she, looking at them with tears in her eyes, "let us thank the good God Who has sent us enough to live upon for more than a week; we had nothing left!"

"And did you hear, mother, what the lady said to the gentleman, that in Paris I would be able to make a great deal of money?"

"Hush, Jean Paul; Paris is too far; never speak again of Paris."

Yes, Paris is very far from Escaladios, very far from those high mountains in the Pyrenees where Jane and her children lived. However, a fortnight after the visit of the ladies, when there was but one piece of money left, Jean Paul repeated: "In Paris, mother, in Paris I could earn enough for you and me to live on. In Paris I should get gold pieces and I would send them to you."

His mother sighed and did not answer.

"There is M. Legras passing," said Jean Paul, suddenly jumping up quickly and running to the road.

He soon joined the good farmer, who stopped a moment to listen to him. But Jean Paul had so many things to say that he begged M. Legras to go on. They descended the hill together. Jean Paul spoke all the time. M. Legras listened. When they reached the fountain they stopped; M. Legras embraced the child, looking at him steadily for some time, then said to him:

"Very well, my boy, I will speak to your mother; you may expect me to-morrow."

"Thank you, Monsieur Legras. Thank you!" said Jean Paul, shaking the farmer's hand with all his might. "To-morrow!"

He ran up the hill and went into the house. His cheeks were burning, his eyes animated, but he spoke no more of Paris. He helped his mother to get ready the scanty supper for the family.

His mother was quite alone the next day when, faithful to his promise, M. Legras entered the little house. Jean Paul was not very far off; he was returning from the fountain, loaded with his heavy pitcher of water. He saw M. Legras go up the hill, and hurrying, he arrived almost at the same time that he did.

Jean Paul's mother was delighted with the visit of this good man, who had so often helped them in their difficulties. As for him, he was quite embarrassed with the joy she showed and with her warm welcome.

"Well! good mother," said he to her as he sat down. "Do not be so glad to see me. Everybody is suffering here. Poor mother! this will be a hard year. Come! keep up your spirits! I have come to ask you to let Jean Paul go to Paris."

The mother ran to Jean Paul, who was standing by M. Legras, pressed him in her arms and covered him with kisses. It seemed as if she wished to say, "Who would dare to take him from my arms?" Jean Paul returned his mother's kisses and wept with her. M. Legras turned away his head; he did not want it to be seen that he was weeping, also.

"Hum! Hum!" said he suddenly, trying to speak gruffly, "you are not reasonable, my dear friend. Do you want your children to die of hunger this winter? Jean Paul is already a big boy; he is strong and courageous; he can gain his livelihood honestly by showing his little animals. Do you know that this winter all the boys of our village are going away to seek their fortune? Callas's son has already gone, as well as Catherine's two sons. Those who stay will be forced to beg their bread before the first snow, and nobody here will have anything to give them."

Jean Paul's mother's only answer was a groan.

"Yes, you are a very good mother, I know it well.

Alas! if the harvest had been good I would not have asked you to part with your son; I should have said to you, 'My good friend, come twice a week to my farm; there will always be a loaf of bread there for you.' But this year I have not enough wheat to feed my own family. I must buy it, and money is scarce."

"Monsieur Legras, you are very good! You have always been good to me and my children, that is the reason I suffer so much when you advise me to let Jean go away. I know that I ought to do as you tell me, and that I must be separated from my boy— but——"

"No, no, my good friend, do not decide so quickly; take time for reflection—he is your child, after all."

He sighed deeply.

"Listen to me," he said, after a moment. "In a week I intend to go to Bagnères; it will be market day then, and I want to pay the rent of my farm. If you consent to let Jean Paul go, he can mount behind me on my horse; that will take him five leagues on his way."

"Thank you, Monsieur Legras; my resolution is taken," she answered in a broken voice. "I feel that God asks this sacrifice. In a week Jean Paul shall start with you."

After M. Legras went, Jean Paul seated himself on his mother's knee, and while caressing her, began to speak of the money which he would send her when he should get to Paris, and the delight of his little sisters, when they should have new dresses and as much white bread as they wanted. His mother did not seem to hear him. "A week," she said suddenly, "only a week! Poor boy, I always hoped to be able to send you to school. All you know is how to pray to God—and if you were to forget Him! If you should be no longer able to say the Lord's Prayer! I will not let you go until you learn to read that beautiful prayer."

She rose up quickly, opened the drawer of the old sideboard, took from it a little bag of brown merino, from which she drew a gold-edged book and kissed it reverently.

"This is your father's prayer book, my poor boy; your father was more learned than I—and—" Her tears were ready to flow, but she restrained them.

"I will give you this book. You shall carry it with you; it will make you remember your father and your mother, but, above all, God Who is both your true Father and true Mother. But before letting you go, I want you at least to learn the Lord's Prayer. Formerly, when I had not so much to do, I made you spell. Do you remember?"

The good little Jean Paul had not forgotten. In a very few days, by pointing out the words with his finger, in his father's book, he could read, "Our Father, Who art in heaven."

A week passed very quickly. His mother, however, passed part of her nights in mending the old clothes of her dear boy who was going to leave her so soon. The eve of his departure had arrived. His little sisters did not know that their brother was going to leave them. Their mother had not had courage enough to tell them of her trouble; but after supper, when both mother and children said their evening prayer together, the mother raised her voice and said, "Let us pray for all travellers, my beloved children; let us ask God to protect those

who are going to take long journeys, and to bring them
back safely to those who love them." Their mother's
voice trembled so much that all her little children were
touched by it, and they raised their hearts to God in
fervent prayer.

They said "good-night" many times, and kissed each
other very often that evening. The little ones went to
bed, but Jean Paul sat up with his mother. She talked
a long time in a sweet low voice to her dear boy, who
was going to leave her. At the same time her skilful
fingers were mending his clothes; at length she had put
in the last stitch. With his mother's help Jean Paul
dressed himself, then he knelt down before her and
said, "Bless me, mother; in a few hours I shall start."

His mother laid her hands on her child's head: "Oh,
my God," she said, "Thou alone canst really bless him!
Bless my child! Thou knowest how my heart is filled
with fear. I dread both accidents and sickness for him.
God, keep them far from him! But I tremble also for
him. O God, I fear both sin and evil; I pray, O Heavenly Father, that Thou wilt keep his soul from all evil,
as well as his body; keep him from temptation and bad
example, from lying and from all vices, and that he
may always love and obey Thee!"

Jean Paul's mother drew him to her and held him a
long time in her arms. "Go to bed," said she; "my
poor boy, you need rest; you will have very little; it is
past midnight." Jean Paul, without undressing, threw
himself on his bed; he shut his eyes, which were swollen
with weeping, and slept. His mother also went to bed,
but not to sleep; however, when day began to break she
felt more calm and not so tired. She had prayed to

God for aid during the last hours of the night; she had told Him all that she suffered, and He had given her resignation and hope.

Before it was quite light she heard in the distance the trotting of a horse. She got up and touched Jean Paul with her hand. He started, rubbed his eyes, jumped from his bed, and collected his little packages. First of all he took the big cage for the mice, well filled with bread and cheese, where my lady and Rosette lived; then the little box which held their dresses; afterward a very white little board which he proudly called his theatre. Under his clothes, on his breast, he placed his precious book, which was fastened with a ribbon around his neck.

M. Legras knocked gently at the door. Jean Paul kissed his little sisters quietly without awaking them, threw himself again in his mother's arms, promising her upon his knees that he never would forget that the good God always saw him; then he opened the door and sprang lightly on the horse behind M. Legras.

"May God bless you, dear little house that I love, and all those who live in it!" said he, sobbing.

He was gone—his mother saw him no more, nor heard any longer even the heavy trot of the big horse. She stood at the door and prayed to God for him with all her heart.

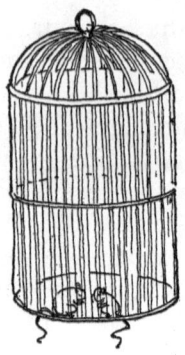

CHAPTER IV

First performance

THE good horse trotted so hard that M. Legras and Jean Paul were well shaken, and he went so fast over the rough road that they arrived at Bagnères before eleven o'clock.

Bagnères is a very pretty town, and therefore Jean Paul, after saying good-bye to M. Legras, stood gaping and admiring the fine churches and houses, as well as the handsome ladies, and splendid shops.

But what is he thinking of? Did he leave home to amuse himself? Has he already forgotten his mother and sisters, whose bread he must gain by his work? And now our good Jean Paul did not waste any more time, but seated himself on the doorsteps, opened the trunk of his little mice and dressed them.

"Halloa! my lady, do you like to travel? And do you like it, Rosette? I give you notice that you are in a very pretty town, where, as they say at our village, a great many fine ladies from Paris come to take the baths and to show their handsome dresses. I want you to do the same. *He, He, He!* we are going to dress ourselves."

Perhaps my lady and Rosette might have liked travelling if they could have walked or gone on horseback, but certainly they did not like travelling shut up in a cage, for they seemed very tired when Jean Paul looked at them through the bars. He took them out carefully one after the other, caressed them and kissed them, then put on their little dresses.

A young lady standing at a window on the opposite side of the street was looking at his proceedings. She made a motion with her finger to another lady, who had just joined her. Both held their napkins in their hands as if they had been interrupted at their meal.

"Do you recognize him?" said the first lady to the second.

"Let me think," said the latter; "where have I seen him? Oh! it is our little boy from Escaladios—and there are the famous mice."

"Little boy! little boy!" she cried out.

Jean Paul raised his head.

"How long since you left Escaladios?"

"This morning, my kind ladies," answered Jean Paul, who had just finished dressing the little creatures.

While speaking, he came near the window where these ladies were. He saw a large room in which was an immense table covered with glasses and plates. They had just finished breakfast; many ladies and gentlemen were still at the table and only a few had left it.

"Would you like to amuse yourself a few minutes?" said the lady who had just spoken to Jean Paul, addressing herself to the people at the table. "If so, tell the waiter to bring in the boy who is at the window."

The order was given. In a few minutes the waiter came into the dining room, holding Jean Paul by the hand; he was quite disconcerted, and blushed a great deal when he was introduced among these fashionable people. The two ladies came to his aid. They cleared off a part of the table and told him to place his mice there.

My lady and Rosette were tired with their journey, and felt the want of moving their little active limbs. So they were more lively and more frolicsome than usual. By degrees, all those who were in the dining room came near the end of the table, where the performance took place, some attracted by the little animals' tricks and others by the mild and intelligent face of the little showman. When the show was over, and the little mice had mounted on Jean Paul's shoulder, he took his red cap off and handed it to each one of the spectators. The sous and other money fell quickly into it; at every new offering, Jean Paul smiled and showed his white teeth. When he came before the lady who had made him come in, she held something between her thumb and second finger. "Before I give you anything," said she, looking mischievously at him, "you must tell me why you have left Escaladios and that kind woman, your mother."

Jean Paul no longer laughed; at the name of his mother the tears blinded his eyes.

"Oh, madam! there is no wheat this year in the moun-

HE TOOK HIS RED CAP OFF AND HANDED IT TO EACH OF THE
SPECTATORS

37

tains, no bread for the poor—we must leave those we love."

The lady let her offering fall into Jean Paul's cap.

The child gave such a jump that all the money he had received rolled on the floor.

"The ten-sous gold piece! it is the same!" said he, taking it between his fingers. "I knew it in a moment, and I recognized you, also, kind madam; you are the lady from the castle of Escaladios. But mother bought bread with this nice piece; how did it come back again into your purse? It was the baker who gave it to you; I understand——"

Everybody laughed—the lady opened her porte-monnaie.

"Look," said she, laughing; "here are plenty like it; there is more than one gold piece in the world, my poor boy. But tell me what you are going to do with the one I have given you?"

"Oh!" replied Jean Paul, "I am going to send it to my mother. My kind lady, if you are going to return to Escaladios to-day, will you take it to her, and tell her that the good God has already blessed Jean Paul?"

The young lady explained to him in a few words that she was going to stay at Bagnères a week longer and then return to Paris.

Jean Paul continued to pass his cap. When he presented it to the last lady, "Look!" said she, throwing into his cap a little five-franc piece, "I want you to know by experience that there is more than one gold piece in the world, and that there are even very small pieces of it; and besides, I love children who work for their mother."

This was too much happiness for Jean Paul; he put his cap upon the table, took his mice in his hands, and began a lively mountain dance, singing lustily. The people in the dining room were amused to see such great joy. Suddenly the child stopped, staggered, and became frightfully pale; a gentleman ran towards him and took him in his arms as he was going to fall.

"It is nothing," said Jean Paul, in a weak voice; "it is joy, I am too happy."

"Too happy!" repeated the young physician who had held him in his arms, and who now made him sit down, while every one surrounded him. "Too happy! joy does not produce these effects. Tell me, my boy, what have you eaten this morning?"

"Nothing at all. It is true, my kind mother put a piece of bread in my pocket: it is there yet, I could not eat it—I was too much troubled."

"But now that you are so happy, you will be able to eat your breakfast. Won't you?" said the physician, smiling. "Put your money in your pocket, and come with me. I am going to take you to the kitchen; the servants are at breakfast, eat as much as you can; a physician prescribes it."

Jean Paul followed the prescription of the physician exactly, and was soon quite well.

By this time it was one o'clock. Jean Paul walked along the dusty road by which he had entered Bagnères in the morning. The sun shone very hot, and his cheeks were like fire. Why did he remain here breathing the burning dust? He expected some one.

He had scarcely left the hotel where he had had

such a good breakfast, when he began to think how
he could send the money to his mother. All at once
he thought, "If M. Legras has not yet gone!" Seized
by a sudden inspiration, he ran to the market place.
But it was all in vain, M. Legras was not there. There
was still another chance of meeting him; he could go
and wait on the same road that they had passed over
this morning. He waited one hour, two hours—the
time seemed very long. M. Legras had doubtless gone
before Jean Paul came there to wait for him. To
amuse himself, he sat down, and began to count his
money; it was very difficult—two pieces of gold, one
smaller than the other, six ten-sous pieces, and nine
big sous.

"I will send them all to my mother," said he to himself; "she will know how to count them."

He was turning his money over and over, rubbing
it with his fingers to make it shine, when suddenly he
heard the trotting of a horse, and at a little distance
saw the honest face of M. Legras, in the midst of a
cloud of dust. Jean Paul gave a cry of joy. M.
Legras stopped his horse.

"Ah! little fellow!" said he, "I see how it is. It
was hardly worth while to start. You want to go
back to your home already."

"No, sir," answered the child, blushing, "I should
like very much to see my mother again, but I am not
going to ask you to take me back. I stopped you to
beg you to take this money to my mother."

The good farmer leaned over his horse and took
the money from Jean Paul.

"How!" said he, counting the money. "More than

nineteen francs already! How did this happen, my boy?"

The good farmer looked suspiciously at Jean Paul.

"Monsieur Legras," said the child, with tears in his eyes, "tell mother that I gained the money honestly, by showing my little mice to travellers at the Hotel de France. Tell her also that Jean Paul would rather die than steal a two-sous piece."

"And what will you have left?" said M. Legras.

"Nothing at all," said Jean Paul simply. "I have had a good breakfast, I do not want anything."

While talking, M. Legras had put into his purse the money that Jean Paul had given him.

"Well, my boy, your mother will have, to-morrow, every sou of the money you have made. Your old friend will give you this piece of money, that you may have something to eat while you are waiting to make more."

He slipped a piece of money into Jean Paul's hand, and putting spurs to his horse, he was already far off.

CHAPTER V

"And lead us not into temptation."

THE next day Jean Paul quitted Bagnères. He did not go by the diligence, nor by the steamboat. He did not go upon a horse or an ass. He took a carriage which cost nothing, and which was always ready: he started off on foot, with his light luggage upon his back, and in this manner he walked the two hundred leagues which separated Bagnères from our great Paris.

We forgot that one evening when he was near Bordeaux, he went six leagues in a fine carriage, and it happened thus:

It had been two months since Jean Paul had quitted Bagnères; he had passed through a great many towns and villages; he had slept upon the straw in a great many barns, and had more than once slept under the trees when he could not reach a house before night. He had dressed and undressed his little white mice very often, he had taken great care of their pretty clothes, he had made them show all they knew--but he had only earned a few sous, which he was obliged to spend. He was very sad this November evening, when he was hurrying along the great highway. He hoped to make some money in the large town of Bordeaux, of which every one talked so much in his country. But he was still very far from it. If he wanted to reach there the next day, he would be obliged to walk all night, and he was already very tired. The road, however, was easy and straight, and the carriages with their fast horses went like the wind. A light carriage drawn by a spirited horse passed by Jean Paul; there was but one man in it, and he half asleep. Jean Paul sighed on looking at the empty place, which he would have liked so much to occupy. The carriage had only gone a short distance when Jean Paul saw something fall from it into the dust. He hurried on and picked it up. It was a little child's coat lined with fur.

"Ho! ho! coachman! stop!" cried Jean Paul, running as fast as he could after the carriage.

"HO! HO! COACHMAN! STOP!" CRIED JEAN PAUL.

But the carriage was so light, and the horse so swift, that the distance between it and Jean Paul increased rapidly. Jean Paul stopped quite out of breath; he thought he could not go another step; he wiped his forehead; he looked at the pretty garment: one would have thought it was made for him. The winter was near, the evenings were cold, and even at this moment, all wet as he was with perspiration, the wind seemed freezing. He put his arm in one of the sleeves, but as soon as he had done so, he drew it out violently.

"Mon Dieu," said he, "let me not yield to temptation!"

And he began to run as fast as he could. The carriage seemed now like a little black spot upon the road.

"Oh, oh! stop!" cried he, although no one could hear him.

"Stop? whom do you want to stop?" said a young peasant on horseback, who was passing at the moment and stopped to speak to him.

"No, it was not you to whom I called," said Jean Paul, still running, "stop! it is the carriage yonder."

"Yonder? nearly at the turn of the road?" replied the young peasant. "Well, you are simple, my child, to think that your little legs can get up to it. It will be as much as I can do on horseback, and Brune goes very fast. Wait; you'll see; I'll stop it."

"Tell the coachman that he has lost——" said Jean Paul.

But the young man did not listen; he put spurs to Brune, and started off with all his might. Jean Paul, although out of breath, continued to run; soon a turn in the road hid both the carriage and the horseman that followed it, but it was not for a very long time. In about a minute after, Jean Paul saw the carriage turn around and come towards him. The coachman was standing up in the carriage, looking in every part of the road for something.

"Here it is! Here it is!" said Jean Paul, holding high the precious coat, so that the person who had lost it might know sooner where to find it.

"Oh, what good luck!" said the coachman, "but where did you find it?"

"Yonder on the road, near the pool," said Jean Paul, still quite out of breath.

"So far off as that?" asked the coachman. "Poor boy you have done me a great service. It is Master Oscar's coat, Madame's dear child. She made me go fifteen leagues to get it, fearing that her little boy would take cold without it. If I had come back without it, I don't know what she would have done to me—Russian furs too! Thank you, my boy! how you have run, my poor child; how red you are, and wet with perspiration! Where are you going in this way, all alone?"

"To Bordeaux," answered Jean Paul, still out of breath.

"To Bordeaux! I am going still farther," replied the coachman. "I will be there this evening at eight o'clock. Jump up here my boy, alongside of me; that will rest you, and you can go much faster than on foot."

Jean Paul had not to be told twice; he sprang lightly into the carriage. The kind coachman wrapped him up carefully in the beautiful fur coat, so that he did not feel the frosty night air.

"Bah! that will not soil it," he muttered in a low voice. "I should not like this nice boy to take cold on my account; he is worth two of that great idler, Master Oscar."

Jean Paul thanked him, but did not speak again; he slept soundly, and did not wake up until the carriage stopped to put him down in the large square at Bordeaux.

Chapter VI

Jean Paul is robbed, but still rich

JEAN PAUL had now been at Bordeaux two weeks, and he did not think of leaving it. He was very happy; he had collected a little money; not that he had received any of those nice gold pieces that he liked so much, but he got a great many little and big sous, and he often asked the baker to change them for silver pieces.

We find him now in the midst of a group of pretty workwomen of Bordeaux. The performance was over, and each one had given him her little offering. Jean Paul was going to undress my lady and her maid, and to take a walk on the fine wharves of Bordeaux, that he thought so pretty; he would see the large river which one might almost think was the sea, and then all the ships which came from the four quarters of the globe.

While thinking of the river and the ships, Jean Paul was packing up his little theatre, and did not remark that a fat gentleman was coming very slowly towards him. He placed himself before the child, leaning on his gold-headed cane, and watched his movements with great interest.

"Instead of undressing the mice, dress them, you ninny!" said some one in Jean Paul's ear. "Do you not see that the gentleman is crazy to see them? Now make them perform, you will be well paid for it."

50

"NOW MAKE THEM PERFORM AND YOU WILL BE WELL PAID FOR IT"

Jean Paul turned around to see who it was that spoke to him. It was a little ragamuffin of about fourteen or fifteen years of age, a stupid-looking fellow with red eyes and a pale and thin face. He was almost naked; through the holes in his shirt and trousers one could see his dirty skin; he had bare feet, and his hair fell in disorder on his forehead and neck. Jean Paul was horrified at his appearance. He followed his advice, however, and prepared quickly for another performance. The old gentleman seemed more and more attentive; he did not take his eyes off my lady and Rosette, and laughed heartily at their pretty tricks. Jean Paul, who had seen them so often, looked now and then at the fat gentleman opposite to him.

Bless me! what did Jean Paul see? Why did he stare so, and look so frightened? Why did he not occupy himself with the little mice? Rosette played badly, my lady made mistakes, the play was a failure. Jean Paul thought he saw a hand sliding under the vest of the old gentleman, and carrying off the big watch-chain and the watch hanging to it. It was the ragamuffin's hand that he saw. "Oh!" cried Jean Paul, quite beside himself, "Help! Thieves! Sir, Sir!"

At these cries the frightened mice jumped into their master's arms; the old gentleman, who did not know what was the matter, turned like a tee-to-tum, the shopkeepers ran out of their shops, all the passers-by surrounded Jean Paul; everybody seemed bewildered except the ragged boy who, at Jean Paul's first cry, threw himself roughly upon him, and said to him in a low voice,

"Fool! you have made us fail in our attempt. Do

you think I care for your ugly animals? I told you
to show them to the rich old man, that while he was
looking at them, I might rob him of his watch and
money. Really, you are more stupid, a thousand times
more so than your mice; you shall pay for it."

Jean Paul wanted to answer him, but the thief had
already run far away. He glided into the crowd like
an eel, and disappeared into a neighboring street.

Meanwhile the tumult continued around Jean Paul.
Everybody spoke at once, and nobody listened. The
old gentleman with the gold-headed cane began to think
it was time to return home; he put his hand in his
watch fob; there was no longer a watch there; he felt
and searched every where for it. Jean Paul, who had
not yet recovered from his agitation, ran to him and
told him all that had happened. The gentleman was
very angry at being robbed, seized our friend by the
collar, and said that it was his fault, and that he would
put him in prison. Fortunately Jean Paul found a
defender in a merchant, who had arrived at his first
scream, and who had seen all; and who would have
caught the thief also, if he had not been prevented
by the great crowd.

"Sir, you ought to be ashamed of yourself to want
to punish this child; on the contrary, you ought to
thank him. If he had not been so honest, you would
not have a sou in your pocket."

" 'Tis true! 'tis true!" they all cried, "he is a fine
boy."

The women embraced him, the men clapped him on
the shoulder, some slipped small pieces of money into
his hand; but by degrees the crowd dispersed, and our

friend was alone. His heart was beating violently, and his eyes were still filled with tears. "I will start from here this evening," said he to himself. "I do not like Bordeaux."

He put his little luggage on his back, tied the money that had been given to him in his handkerchief. "So much more to add to my hoard!" said he to himself. "As soon as I have twenty francs I will send it to my mother!"

He jumped about, he was again gay, he forgot the sad scene that he had just passed through. He went into a baker's, then to a pork butcher's shop. He must eat meat to-day, he wanted all his strength, as he was going to travel. He was in the middle of the long bridge of Cubjac, which crossed the Dordogne, and he was taking a farewell look at the wharves, the boats, and the river, when three persons approached him, for whom he was obliged to stand on one side to let them pass; there were·two policemen, and between them Jean Paul recognized the young thief.

"They are taking him to prison," said Jean Paul. "What will his poor mother say!"

The thief did not see him at first; he only recognized him the moment that he passed him.

"Well, great ninny!" he cried as soon as he recognized him, "you have very little wit for your age. Well! tell me," and he began to laugh with all his might; "where are all those nice ten-sous pieces that were in your pocket? look for them; they are all in my eye," and he laughed still louder. "That will teach you, my boy, not to meddle with those who are more knowing than you."

Jean Paul had put his hand quickly in his pocket. The precious little bag of coarse linen, that held his money, was gone. He ran to the policemen and told them of his loss, and begged them to make the wicked boy give him his money, which he had had so much trouble to earn, and that he wanted to send to his mother. The policemen told him that when they had arrested the boy, they had searched, and found nothing on him.

"Nothing in my hands! nothing in my pockets!" said the little rascal. "Ah! M. Ninny, when you began to scream so, and I threw myself on you, you did not feel my hand in your pocket. That was the way of it. I did it well, there is no use crying about it."

The policemen had great trouble to make him hush, and then went off with him.

Our friend Jean Paul remained motionless; he could not believe his eyes. At last he threw himself upon the ground and burst out sobbing.

"Oh, the wicked boy! what a bad heart he has! the rascal who has robbed me of my mother's money! I am glad that he has been taken! I am glad that he will be put in prison! I hope he will remain there——"

Jean Paul did not finish; he thought he saw the prison, a dark, cold, damp dungeon, still as death, nobody near the prisoner, he is alone; God who consoles the afflicted, will not console him, because he has done wrong.

"Oh, I will not curse him," said Jean Paul, "he is more unhappy than I am."

He stopped a moment and then began again: "And

My lady and Rosette

if I had helped him to-day to steal, I would have been arrested and taken to prison also." He shuddered.

"It was my good mother who taught me not to do wrong. This unfortunate boy has perhaps never known a mother's care. Oh God! I thank Thee for thy protection this day! I forgive him from the bottom of my heart. Do Thou forgive him also; console him in his sad prison. Make him weep, make him repent of his faults, and then make him happy in being loved by Thee!"

Jean Paul got up. His head was light again. Night was coming on. He sent a kiss to the stars, where he thought God's throne was. Jean Paul always loved the good God. He leaped for joy, then he set out on his journey.

Chapter VII

Jean Paul buys a bed and sheets

THE way was long from Bordeaux to Paris. Jean Paul never liked to speak of this part of his journey; he said one day was so much like another, and he was sometimes so tired he could not bear to think of it.

He arrived there at length. It was toward the end of the month of January. It was more than four months since he had left the dear little house in Escaladios. It was evening when he reached the great city; all the lamps and shops were lighted. There was a busy crowd going and coming as if it was in the middle of the day. He was elbowed and jostled every moment. He stopped, his heart shrank within him.

58

"In this immense crowd," said he to himself, "nobody loves me, nobody cares for me. Oh, dear little house in the Pyrenees, when shall I see you again?"

A porte-cochère was open near him; it was an old door of an old house. At the end of the yard pieces of stuff were hanging on a line to dry. It was a dyer's, as could be easily seen by two black streams, and a disagreeable smell.

Jean Paul sheltered himself in the doorway, glad to be away from the crowd and the noise of the carriages which stunned him. He leaned against a post, hid his head in his hands, and began to cry. He did not hear the door open behind him, but a strong smell of fried onions made him lift up his head. A little thin sallow man was looking at him.

"What are you doing here," said he roughly, "and what are you crying for?"

"Mother," muttered Jean Paul.

"What is that you are mumbling?" said the little man. "Why don't you answer?" and he shook him by the sleeve. "What are you doing here, and what are you crying for?"

"I do not know."

"Well, here is a queer child, who is sobbing ready to break his heart, and he does not know why. Be off with you!"

"I would rather remain here," said Jean Paul.

"No, I tell you that is impossible," said the little man, who began to be impatient; "the carriages coming in the yard will crush you against the wall."

"Then you will not let me sleep here?" said Jean Paul.

"Sleep here!" said the little man; "such weather as this, with this freezing wind which would cut you in two!" He shivered. "Are you crazy? you would be dead to-morrow morning. Off with you, with your nonsense! Go home quick!"

"But I have no home, I do not know where to go," stammered Jean Paul.

"Ah! you do not know where to go? you are a vaga-bond, a rascal. The policemen will take you, and put you in prison! Go away from here, you beggar!"

"I am not a beggar," said Jean Paul sadly, but with a certain pride, "I gain my livelihood honestly. Let me sleep in your doorway, my good sir; no harm will come to me. For more than two months I have passed the night——"

"Well! you are going to take cold again in this porte-cochère, and in this horrid draught!" cried a big fat woman who came out of the lodge. "Let us see what it is? Make the boy come in, and talk to him in the room; but do not freeze yourself there."

"Make him come in, indeed! I want him to go away," cried the little man. "Off with you, quick!"

But the big woman had pushed both her husband and the child into the room, and had carefully shut the door; then she pointed her finger at the husband, to show him something that was cooking over the fire, and put a big wooden spoon in his hand.

"Come, Monsieur Fumeron," said she to him, "make yourself useful; keep the stew from burning; and do keep quiet, nobody can understand anything."

The little husband, grumbling, seated himself by the fire, and began stirring the stew. The big woman put her arms a-kimbo, fixed herself in front of Jean Paul, looked in his face, and began to question him.

There was so much goodness in her fresh and chubby face that, in spite of her fierceness, Jean Paul told her all his story. When he had finished, the little husband jumped up quickly, threw the big spoon on the table, and said, "Well, since he has come all the way from the Pyrénées, and he has walked two hundred leagues, that shows his legs are good, and that he can leave here, and go somewhere else."

"For shame, Monsieur Fumeron! you are getting very cruel," said the fat woman. "Hold your tongue; you ought to be ashamed to speak so."

She took her husband by the arm, and led him to the corner of the room, where she talked to him in a low voice and with animation. M. Fumeron shook his head, and did not seem pleased.

"Are you really a fool, Madame Fumeron?" cried he, stamping with his foot suddenly. "I tell you he is a beggar, a vagabond. Foh! you do not know what you are saying."

"But I do know what I am saying, and—well, we shall see."

She came back quickly to Jean Paul, and said to him in a hurried voice,

"In Paris, my child, people are not allowed to sleep in the street. Every one must have a home and pay for it: that is what is called paying your rent. Have you any money?" Jean Paul said that he had.

"Well, then, you can lodge in what is called a fur-nished room, a big chamber where ten or twenty un-

fortunate people sleep pell-mell; it will cost you two
or three sous a day; will you be able to pay that?"

"Yes, I believe so," said Jean Paul, in a low voice;
he did not feel inclined to sleep pell-mell with twenty
unfortunates.

"Well, then, since you are so rich," looking at her
husband triumphantly, "I will not let you go to one of
those places, where you will be likely to meet robbers
and murderers. We have at the top of the house a
little closet."

"But I tell you, wife, that closet is too small for
a bed," said M. Fumeron.

"We are not speaking of a bed," replied Mme.
Fumeron—"the child is not big. A good bundle of
straw will do, won't it?" said she, looking at Jean
Paul. "Hush then! Monsieur Fumeron, you are always talking, you interrupt me always; one can hear
nothing but your voice. You make me lose the thread
of my discourse."

She began again. "A little room, which we will
rent to you for two sous a day, and where you can
come and sleep every night. Do you hear, Monsieur
Fumeron? It is settled."

Jean Paul threw his arms around the fat woman.

"How good you are! Thank you! thank you! Then
I may sleep here, in this house?"

"You must pay me a week in advance," said M.
Fumeron, who came near Jean Paul and held out
his hand.

Jean Paul was glad now to give him his big sous.

"Monsieur Fumeron, you are as greedy as a vulture,
I am ashamed of you," said Mme. Fumeron. "If you

choose you may pay your two sous for to-night, but
not a farthing more. Do you hear? and now sit down,
and I will give you a plate of soup (that will teach you
to be avaricious again, Monsieur Fumeron), a piece
of bread and a little stew (that will teach you to be
hard with little children, Monsieur Fumeron), and a
drink of wine. I want my lodger to like me! O! now
I have a lodger!" cried the fat woman, clapping her
hands; "I drink your health, my boy, my lodger!"
She poured out a little wine in Jean Paul's glass, and
took about as much herself, and they both clinked
their glasses. "There," she said to the child when he
had done eating, "now I must shut the big gate; it is
late."

She returned into the room shivering. "Oh, how
cold it is this evening! Monsieur Fumeron, if any
one rings you must pull the string. I positively forbid
you to put your nose out of doors; you will have your
cold again do you hear? Now follow me, my child."

She lighted a candle, crossed the yard, followed by
Jean Paul, and they climbed a narrow staircase together. Jean Paul followed her, followed her, until
he began to ask himself if he was going to climb all
night, when Mme. Fumeron turned into a long entry.
They had now reached the sixth story above the main
floor.

Mme. Fumeron opened the door with a big key, and
Jean Paul saw a little square room completely empty.
The starry sky could be seen through a very small
window. The walls were whitewashed, and pretty
clean. Jean Paul, easily pleased, was enchanted with
his new lodging.

"Oh! but I was foolish to forget the bundle of straw we should have begun with that; it is too cold for you to sleep on the floor. There is plenty of straw in the shop opposite, but we must go down and up again," said the fat woman, leaning against the wall, panting like an ox. "Oh, I can do no more."

Jean Paul did not mind either going down or coming up. When Mme. Fumeron explained to him where he could buy the straw, he put down his luggage and his dear little mice in his new room, then he ran along the corridor, and groped his way in the dark, down stairs. Very soon Mme. Fumeron heard him jumping up the steps four at a time.

A few minutes afterwards, she heard the straw rubbing against the walls of the narrow entry, and saw Jean Paul appear half hidden by his big bundle of straw.

"Now, let us take away the candle. Take care not to set any thing on fire. I will tell you at once, that you must always go to bed without a light! Now go to bed, little fellow; see, you can cover yourself up in this nice fresh straw without undressing yourself. There, half for the bed and half for the cover, and you will sleep like a king."

It was true; the child, after thanking God for the new friend He had sent him, slept like a king—better than many kings. The poor often sleep better on straw than the rich on the softest down.

Chapter VIII

Good cabbages, and bad heart

THE next day our friend began his walks about the great city. In the faubourg Saint Marceau, where he lived, there were more poor than rich people, so Jean Paul, after having run over it all day, brought home but a small sum of money. On his return in the evening, he knocked timidly at the glass door of the good concierge. The honest woman opened the sliding glass; Jean Paul offered her the two-sous piece.

"Oh, it's my little lodger," said she, laughing. "Come in, my boy, and warm yourself. Here is a piece of beef with turnips, which was left from our dinner; you will enjoy it."

Indeed, Jean Paul's nice white teeth soon devoured it, although he thought that he heard M. Fumeron coughing behind the closely shut curtains, grumbling, and saying that he would like nothing better the next day than the beef warmed again.

"Don't mind, my little friend," said the fat woman; "it's only Monsieur Fumeron, whom I sent to bed early, he coughs so much; good night, my boy."

It was just the same the next day. Jean Paul was afraid to go far from the street where he lived, for fear of being lost in the streets, and he made very little money. On coming in at nightfall he knocked at the door of the lodge. It was M. Fumeron this time, who beckoned for him to come in. There was a strong smell of cabbage in the room. The little man was washing and putting away the pots, and the things that had been used at dinner. He had a brown dish in his hand, upon which was some cabbage and a piece of pork, and he was going to put it away in the cupboard.

Jean Paul came to him, and offered him his two sous.

"Oh!" said the little man, turning roughly towards him. "Do you want to make fun of me? Do you think, little vagabond, that I want you to come here every evening, with your big sous in your hand, and eat all our provisions? Ah, little beggar! you thought you would find Madame Fumeron here, and something good to eat; no, Madame is out,,and it is Monsieur who is here to receive you, and he is master here." He looked all around to be sure that his wife did not hear him. "Yes, I am master, and I forbid you to enter here. Do you hear?" While speaking, M. Fumeron pinched Jean Paul's ear with one hand, while with the other he still held the savory dish.

"But," the child said trembling, "my rent? How can I pay my rent?"

"Every month—no, every two weeks, you must bring me thirty sous when you come down in the morning. Do you understand? And now be off with you! I want neither to hear nor to see you any more!"

He let go of Jean Paul's ear, and put the plate of pork and cabbage on the shelf of the cupboard. Jean Paul did not want to be told twice to go away—he opened and shut the door of the lodge, crossed the yard, ran up the staircase like a cat, and was soon in his room wrapped up in his bundle of straw. Our friend had counted a little upon the good supper of Mme. Fumeron, and went to bed with an empty stomach; he felt still more hungry as his appetite had been sharpened by the smell of the pork and cabbage. However, after a while he slept soundly.

Sleep soundly, Jean Paul, the good God loves you; for before you slept, you had promised yourself, if you ever should have a good dish of pork and cabbage, you would give some of it to poor little hungry children.

Jean Paul awoke early the next morning: his first thought was to run to the baker's and buy a big piece of bread.

"It is scarcely light," said he, looking out of his little window. "Seven o'clock has just struck. Madame Fumeron will not get up for an hour yet, the doors will not be open, and the baker will not yet have taken down the shutters of his shop! I am so hungry, I cannot wait any longer," and he put his hands on his empty stomach. "Bah!" said he suddenly, "I am not the first who has suffered from hunger; plenty of others beside me are suffering. If I were sure that my mother and sisters were not suffering, I think I could support my pain patiently. It has been so long since I sent them anything," he went on. "Since I was robbed at Bordeaux I have just earned enough to live! I, who promised them money, and a great deal too! Mother, what do you think of your Jean Paul? Do you think he has forgotten you? Mother, I've done all that you told me to do. There, in its case,

is my father's book, hanging from a nail. I take it
with me every Sunday to church. I don't open it; I
don't need it, for I know the prayer you taught me;
I have said it so often since I left you! No, I don't
open the dear book, but I kiss it while thinking of God,
of my father who is with God, and of you, darling
mother. Oh mother! I hope that you have not suffered from hunger since I left you, nor my dear little
sisters. Oh mother, I want to see you so much again!''

The tears came to the eyes of the poor child, he
began to sob, when he heard a slight noise at his door.
He listens—he is not mistaken—some one has turned
the key. Jean Paul jumped up quickly, shook the stalks
of straw off, which were sticking to his clothes, and
called out,

"Who is there? Come in," said he. There was no
answer. He opened the door; nobody was there, the
entry was empty.

"It's the wind," said he to himself.

Just then it struck eight o'clock. Jean Paul ran
rapidly down stairs, and in a moment was at the baker's.

In the evening he ran past the lodge, and did not
appear to hear Mme. Fumeron who was calling him.

Chapter IX

Where Madeleine appears

THE next morning Jean Paul had just got up and was stooping to give some crumbs of bread to my lady and Rosette, when he heard again a noise at his door, the key moving in the key-hole.

"Come in," cried Jean Paul, "come in!"

He got up and ran to the door. Nobody was there. The entry was empty from one end to the other.

The following day the same noise at the door, the same "Come in," from Jean Paul, the same silence, and no one in the entry, when he went to the door. But that day, Jean Paul had seen the key turn in the lock, he was sure of it. "It's not the wind," he said: "I will see you to-morrow, no matter who it is; yes, I will see you!"

So when he had just got up the next morning, he posted himself near the door. With one hand he held the latch, so that at the least noise he might open it.

He had stood there a quarter of an hour; there was no sound; all was quiet. Jean Paul began to feel tired, and he was just going, as he did every morning, to attend to his little household. "I will wait one moment longer here," he said to himself; for he thought he heard the door of the next chamber open, then light footsteps, and something brushing against the wall, then some one touched the key. He turned the latch quickly, and opened the door. Jean Paul received a hard knock upon his head, and screamed out. There was also another scream, and a little girl nearly fell upon him.

"You hurt me," said Jean Paul, rubbing his forehead.

"You hurt me, too," said the little girl, who looked very red, was nearly crying, and at the same time rubbing her forehead.

"I didn't know that you were leaning against the door, I didn't wish to hurt you," said our friend. "You nearly fell when I opened the door, and your head knocked against mine. It wasn't my fault. But it doesn't hurt me any more," said the good little Jean Paul, smiling, "and you? Your forehead is still quite red!"

"Oh, it's better now," said the little girl, smiling also. "But what made you open your door so quickly?"

"If I had known that you were leaning against it, I would not have done so, you may be sure! But now I must tell you, that for two or three mornings lately, some one has stopped, and tried the door as if they wished to come in but as soon as I said: Who is there?——"

"But," interrupted the little girl, in a sweet voice, "I can assure you I did not want to come in. That was the reason that I was afraid and ran away, as soon as you said, 'Come in.' To-day you did not say anything, so I——" she stopped and blushed.

"Then it was you who came every morning to my door! But why did you do so, if you didn't want to come in?"

"I—I——" the little girl hesitated.

Let us look at her while she is silent. She appeared to be about ten years old; she had a sweet and intelligent face; her large honest brown eyes showed that she was truthful; her round and rosy cheeks, that she was healthy; and her light hair so smoothly arranged on her forehead, that she had a good mother who loved and took great care of her. She was dressed in a very clean calico dress, with a black apron.

"I—I——" she resumed, "was looking through the key-hole to see the little white mice. I'll tell you all about it," she added quickly. "My name is Madeleine Bienfait. My father and mother live in the room next to yours. I am an apprentice to a mantua-maker. Last Monday, my mistress sent me to buy some thread; in going along the streets, I saw your little mice playing. I stopped for two minutes only, fearing to be scolded. The same evening I saw you come in, and go up stairs before me, and now that I have found out that the little white mice are my neighbors, you see, I am dying to see them again."

"Why did you not say so, Mademoiselle Madeleine? It would have been so easy for me to have shown them to you. Well, you shall see them to-day—now. I

am going to show you what I call a grand performance;" and he began at once to get ready.

"Madeleine! Madeleine! where are you? It is past
eight o'clock, Madeleine!" some one called from the
next room.

"I am here, mother!" cried the little girl. "What
is your name?" said she quickly to Jean Paul.

"Jean Paul," he answered.

"Well, Jean Paul, you can show me the performance to-morrow. Won't you? I will come earlier
than I did to-day, and we will not lose any time. Now
I must go to my work; I am late already."

"Good-bye, Madeleine; remember—to-morrow."

"Good-bye, Jean Paul."

Jean Paul heard the door of the next room open,
then he recognized Madeleine's voice, as she spoke to
her mother, and then he heard the sound of a kiss.

Jean Paul sighed, for he remembered at that moment his mother's kisses.

"Good-bye, Jean Paul," said Madeleine again, as she
passed with her basket on her arm, before the half-
open door of our friend.

"To-morrow, to-morrow!" said Jean Paul.

It was not quite light the next morning when Madeleine knocked loudly at Jean Paul's door. Our friend
opened it with great care this time: all was ready for
the promised play. The theatre was raised from the
floor, and the little animals were dressed; as soon as
Madeleine came in, the performance began. At first
the little girl opened her eyes, and said nothing. Then
she began to laugh so much, and so loud, that Jean
Paul asked her what the neighbors would say.

"Oh, it's only mamma that can hear us," said Madeleine; "she knows that I am here, and it always pleases her very much when I am amused."

Just then, the children were interrupted by a little knock on the partition wall. A voice said,

"Enough, Madeleine! It is eight o'clock; you must go to your work."

"What a pity!" said Madeleine; but she rose quickly.

"Come again to-morrow, come every morning," said Jean Paul to her as she left.

"Oh yes, we enjoy ourselves so much!" said Madeleine.

CHAPTER X

The Chestnuts of the Luxembourg

FOR many weeks the children met every morning to play with my lady and Rosette. Sometimes they did not pay much attention to the charming little animals: Jean Paul related his history to Madeleine; he spoke of his mother and sisters; Madeleine listened attentively, with her large brown eyes fixed upon him. At once she loved the house at Escaladios, his mother, and the dear little girls. Then he told the history of his long journey, of the thief at Bordeaux, and the good Mme. Fumeron.

"How much have you made since you have been in Paris?" Madeleine said one day to him.

"Not much; some days eight sous. It is very sad
—I can put nothing away for my mother."

Madeleine thought a moment.

"If you were to go to the Tuileries, or to the Champs
Elysées, or to some of those pleasant places where there
are so many little children, I'm sure that you would
make more."

"Yes, but how can I get there? I don't know the
way. I should lose myself in this big Paris."

"That is true," said Madeleine thoughtfully.

"Oh, I have thought of something!" cried she, suddenly. "I go every day to a mantua-maker's in the
rue Bonaparte, to work; it is very near a handsome
garden called the Luxembourg. Look," said she, showing him the clear sky and bright sun through the narrow window. "Look! it is going to be clear to-day,
and it is not very cold. The Luxembourg will be full
of children. You will make a. heap of money there,
as big as yourself. I can go with you to a great square,
from which you will be able to see the big trees—
No, I would rather take you to the garden gates, that's
more sure, and it will not delay me five minutes. Then
this evening, when the keepers of the garden make
every one leave it, you can wait on the pavement before
the gate, and we can go home together. It must be
so! it is settled!" said the little girl, clapping her hands.
"Quick, quick! let's dress the ladies. We've done
nothing but talk this morning. Take Rosette, and I'll
dress my lady."

Ten minutes after, Jean Paul and his friend went
out of the old house together, in fine spirits.

Madeleine was not mistaken; the weather was de-

lightful the whole day; it froze a little, but the sun
shone pleasantly. The wide walk of the Luxembourg
was filled with children of all ages, who ran, jumped,
played, and were so happy this fine winter day. Nearly
all of them stopped in front of our friend, forgetting
their jumping ropes and hoops, to look at my lady and
Rosette. It was in vain that their mothers and nurses
called them; they were deaf. Those who answered the
calls held out their hands and asked for some sous,
and as soon as they had received them, they ran back
and gave them to Jean Paul and the little mice. A
little fellow three or four years old, dressed in velvet
and furs, who, when he held his little dimpled hand
to his nurse, received a hard slap from her, with "Let
me alone sir, you trouble me," returned resolutely to
Jean Paul, and emptied out his little pocket on the
stage: it contained a piece of bread, a stick of chocolate which his little teeth had already bitten, and some
pebbles. The little fellow laughed, and then ran off
as fast as his legs could carry him, and hid himself in
the crowd of fair and dark heads.

At length night came; the garden was shut. Jean
Paul seated himself upon the pavement near the gate,
and waited, as it was agreed, for Madeleine. He took
a piece of brown bread from his cap and began to eat
it. It had been a long time since the boy had eaten
his lunch. The white mice were not forgotten; he
gave them their share of the crumbs, and talked to
them affectionately. His heart was filled with joy.
His pocket felt very heavy, but he awaited the arrival
of Madeleine, as he wanted her to have the pleasure
of counting the money he had made. "How glad she

will be!" he said to himself. Meanwhile it became very cold. Jean Paul got up, and walked along the pavement, stamping his feet upon the flagstones. Suddenly he felt a little hand placed upon his shoulder; he turned around, it was Madeleine. He took her hand, and they crossed the street together.

"Come," said he, "you shall see!" He stopped before the little shop of a chestnut-seller, and by the light of the lantern, took his sous one by one from his pockets.

"Count," said he to Madeleine.

Madeleine counted.

"Forty-eight sous!" said she at last; "two francs and eight sous. A good day's work! Sir, will you give us two silver pieces for this?" holding a handful of sous to the chestnut-seller.

"Give the little girl two sous worth of very hot chestnuts too," added Jean Paul, handing a double sous to the shopkeeper.

"No," said Madeleine to the man, "he must take care of his money."

"Yes," said Jean Paul.

"No."

"Yes."

The seller began to laugh; but he arranged the matter, by giving a handful of chestnuts to Madeleine, and giving the two sous back to Jean Paul.

"How good people have been to us to-day!" said Jean Paul. "Dear little Madeleine, it is to you that I owe all this good fortune."

The two children went home even more gayly than they started in the morning. Jean Paul wanted Madeleine to eat all the chestnuts; he said he was not hungry. Madeleine seemed to consent, and shelled them carefully; then she put them in Jean Paul's mouth and nearly choked him; they laughed very much, and there was no end to their jokes. When they had finished eating the chestnuts, they spoke of the two twenty-sous pieces.

"I want you to keep them for me, little Madeleine," said Jean Paul. "When there are enough we will send them to my mother."

Madeleine promised to give them to her mother, who would lock them up carefully.

The two children had now reached Jean Paul's chamber door.

"Adieu, adieu."

"Good night, and to-morrow."

Then they separated.

Chapter XI

Jean Paul acts as nurse

ONE morning, two days after, Madeleine went in to see Jean Paul.

"You are crying," said he, on seeing her swollen eyes and pale face.

"Yes," said Madeleine whose eyes were full of tears. "Yesterday the rheumatism came back in father's legs."

"What is rheumatism?" asked Jean Paul.

"It is a frightful pain," Madeleine answered, "which makes one suffer day and night, and which prevents one from moving."

"Oh, what a horrid sickness!" said Jean Paul.

"The doctor came yesterday. He said that if papa remained at home as he did last year his rheumatism would last three months, for poor papa was very sick last year; but if he went to the hospital, he would be cured in two weeks. Then mamma and I both began to cry, and declared that we would not let papa leave us. But papa answered that he would go to the hospital, that he might be cured sooner; so last evening they took him away. Put your theatre away, Jean Paul; I cannot laugh, and can only think of poor papa."

"But he will be well taken care of, won't he?" said Jean Paul, looking very unhappy.

"O yes! the doctor said that he would have vapor

baths, and thirty-six remedies that we could not give
him at home. But it is all the same; poor papa is suffering, and he is far away from mother, and his little
Madeleine!"

Just then Mme. Bienfait's little clock struck eight.
Madeleine heard it, wiped her eyes, kissed Jean Paul,
and left his room.

The next day was Sunday—a fête day.

Madeleine stayed but a minute with Jean Paul, and
would not play with the mice. She told Jean Paul that
sick persons at the hospital could be seen only on Sunday, and that she was going with her mother to see her
father.

"Oh! how glad I should be," said Jean Paul, "if you
were to find him cured!"

"Cured! that is impossible," said the gentle Madeleine; "if he only suffers a little less! I will tell you all
about it to-morrow."

The Sunday before Lent, always a fête day, was a
sad day for them. It froze so hard, that the water of
the streams was as solid as marble. The sky was dark,
and at about twelve o'clock, big flakes of snow began
to fall so fast that the air was darkened by them.

Jean Paul went to church, then came back to his little
room, where he remained sadly all day. In such
weather it was impossible to go out with my lady and
Rosette.

The next morning he awaited the arrival of his dear
Madeleine with great impatience. It was daylight, and
Madeleine had not yet come, and she did not come. He
ran out of his room, and determined to knock very
softly at Mme. Bienfait's door. He knocked two or

three times; there was no answer, and the key was taken away. He ran quickly down stairs; Mme. Fumeron would doubtless be able to tell him where Madeleine was, and also to give him news of her father; he saw Madeleine in the porte-cochère talking to a young girl a little older than herself. Jean Paul came near them, but the girls were so busy that they did not notice him. "If you could have only stayed to-day with mamma!" said Madeleine. "Poor mamma! she took cold yesterday in returning from the hospital, and she is so delicate! To-day she is in bed with a burning fever, and her cough is very troublesome. I am afraid that she is going to be ill, so I did not wish to leave her this morning; but she got angry—she who is never angry!—I am sure it is the effect of the fever. She declares positively that I must go to my work to-day, that my mistress wanted me, that if I did not go to the workshop when there was a great deal of work they would send me away as soon as there was less, and that I should never learn my trade. She spoke so earnestly, that I did not dare to disobey her; and I pretended to start. But I cannot leave my dear mamma all alone, ill as she is. O, dear Marie, I beg you to stay with her to-day—only to-day!" said Madeleine, crying.

"I tell you that it is impossible, dear Madeleine, quite impossible. In our shop we are overrun with work; we work every night. Just fancy! my mistress has seven dresses to finish for the princess Poupoutoff. They must be ready for the grand ball on Shrove Tuesday. The princess intends changing her costume seven times during the ball. What do you think of that? Formerly, you know each lady had one dress;

but now it is necessary to have seven dresses at one time—and such dresses! There are pearls, ruffles, lace and feathers. There is no end to it. Are these ladies happy, do you think?"

"Happy because they have many dresses! do you think so, Marie? I have but two dresses, one for every day and one for Sunday, and I would gladly give away both of them, if papa and mamma were well; and if it would do any good, I would gladly wear my petticoat and short gown all the winter."

"What you say is true, Madeleine; their fine dresses do not make them happy," answered Marie, thoughtfully. "The other day I carried a skirt to the princess's house; they made me wait more than an hour in a sort of vestibule. On one side, I heard the prince and princess quarrelling; on the other, the children were fighting; and below, the housekeeper was scolding the servants."

"What do I care for this princess?" interrupted Madeleine. "Poor mamma! what is to be done? She is so agitated, I dare not go in again; seeing me would increase her fever. She would say to me again, as she did this morning, 'Go away to your work, go!' I asked Madame Fumeron to stay with her a little while, but she cannot leave the lodge, because Monsieur Fumeron is sick with his catarrh. Oh! what shall I do?"

"I will stay with her, Madeleine; only give me the key. The door is locked; I will take good care of her; I won't let the fire go out; I will give her her warm drinks, and I will be very quiet. Do as your mother tells you, and go to your work, and do not be uneasy; she will be as well taken care of as if you were there."

It was our friend Jean Paul who had approached Madeleine, and, while speaking to her, was wiping the tears from her eyes with the back of his hand.

"Do not cry, do not cry," said he.

"Oh," said Madeleine, after a moment's silence; "you are very good, but I cannot let you stay all day with mamma. This is the Monday before Lent. The big ox will parade the streets. Everybody will be out. Look how bright the sky is! You will make a great deal of money to-day by showing your little animals. I cannot let you lose the whole day."

"Oh, Madeleine, it is not losing the day when I pass it in nursing your mother. Trust to me, and give me the key at once. When my sister Angela was sick, I stayed with her for hours, and my mother said that I took good care of her."

Madeleine at last took the key from her pocket, and gave it to Jean Paul, telling him again and again what he must do for the dear invalid.

Jean Paul ran up the high staircase. When he reached the room, he was surprised to find that Madeleine, who, he thought, had left the house, was behind him. She looked at the dear sick one and blew a kiss to her, although her mother could not see it. Then she nodded to Jean Paul and went off quietly.

When she came back in the evening, quite out of breath from walking so fast, she found her mother asleep. Jean Paul told Madeleine that her mother had coughed a good deal during the day, and had often asked for a drink; she appeared astonished at first to see Jean Paul, but the few words that he spoke to her seemed to quiet her.

"What a good thing it was that I was here this freezing cold weather, that I could give her warm drinks!"

Madeleine thanked him, and they ate some provisions together that they found in the cupboard.

"Thank you, my good Jean Paul; now go to bed; to-morrow we shall meet again. I am going to sit up to-night."

"Sit up, you! Madeleine! after having taken those two long walks! But you must not think of it. Why, your eyes are nearly shut already; no, go to your little bed and sleep soundly. I will stay by the fire to-night; I am not tired. I have not stirred all day. Do not be uneasy, but sleep well, Madeleine."

Just then Mme. Bienfait woke up, coughed, and asked for a drink. Jean Paul gave her a cup of herb tea, and Madeleine kissed her, and asked her how she felt.

"Well, well, my child," answered the poor woman, who soon became drowsy again.

Madeleine rose early; she ran in quickly and insisted upon Jean Paul's taking a few hours of sleep. He did not consent to it, until after she had promised to wake him at eight o'clock, when she would be about leaving.

Madeleine hoped to be able to remain with her mother all day; but when the day broke she wakened, and said to Madeleine with feverish agitation:

"What! have you not started yet! Why, my dear child, you must go to your work. I have promised it— you must go. When I make a promise, I keep it."

She turned herself in her bed, talked to herself, coughed, and refused to take another drink. Madeleine promised to set off at eight o'clock as usual. Her mother seemed to be dozing again, and Madeleine thought she would not leave her, but when eight o'clock struck Mme. Bienfait started. "Eight o'clock," she cried; "you must go. Go, go," repeated she, sitting up in her bed, "I never fail in my promises."

Madeleine forced her to lie down again, then with a very full heart, said good-bye, went out, and woke Jean Paul.

"I am going to the doctor's to beg him to come and see her," she said to him when she left. "There is something left to eat in the cupboard. Poor Jean Paul, how good you are! It is a sad Shrove Tuesday that I am going to make you pass. If the doctor comes while I am away, you will listen and remember what he says, won't you? You will find the herb tea ready made in the teapot, and there is still enough wood in the bottom of the closet. How cold it is!" said she, as she went away slowly. It was so hard for her to leave her dear mother.

Jean Paul slipped very quietly into the sick chamber, and remained there faithfully all day. In the evening some one knocked at the door. It was the doctor; he examined Mme. Bienfait very attentively; then he told Jean Paul that her complaint was bronchitis, and that she required a great deal of care.

"The fire must be kept up night and day, my boy, and do not let her uncover herself; even with a fire, it is cold in these garrets."

"And if I take very good care of her?" said Jean Paul, questioning the doctor with his eyes.

"If you take very good care of her, my friend, she will be cured in a week."

"Oh! thank you, thank you, sir!" said Jean Paul, and he took the doctor's hand and kissed it.

The next day passed in the same way. Madeleine started off a little after eight o'clock, leaving Jean Paul to take care of her mother.

Jean Paul was very much worried. He had burnt all the wood that he had found in the closet, as well as that which the wood dealer had brought. This cross man had grumbled so much when Madeleine, after searching her mother's drawer and not finding any money, had told him that she would pay him soon, as soon as possible, that Jean Paul did not dare to tell his friend that there were but two more sticks! the poor boy took the tongs, looked amongst the ashes for the little pieces of coal, and put them all in a heap one upon another. He must keep those two precious sticks for the night.

But He whom the winds and seas obey, came to Jean Paul's aid. Suddenly the weather changed. The beautiful trees of ice that the frost had drawn upon the windows, began to disappear and run in little streams drop by drop on the floor. It was no longer freezing weather. The sky was dark, and a warm rain was falling.

The invalid's room was warm although the fire was almost out, and she seemed to enjoy this mild air. She did not cough and her breathing became more calm; her cheeks were no longer burning with fever, and she slept quietly.

Jean Paul did not make the fire up again; he said to himself, "She is better already. The doctor said she would get well and she will be cured. Dear God! I thank Thee. This fine weather is better than fire or herb tea."

Madeleine came back, so wet, so muddy, but so happy!

"She is much better," said Jean Paul, as soon as she opened the door.

Madeleine did not answer; she knelt down by the bedside, and kissed her mother's hand again and again. From her inmost heart, she also thanked God.

"You do not know, Jean Paul," she said in a low voice, "that I can stay at home all day to-morrow. I will take care of her to-morrow."

"How is that?" said Jean Paul.

"When I reached the workroom this morning my eyes looked so red, that my mistress took notice of them; you see, Jean Paul, last evening, Shrove Tuesday, all those troublesome dresses of gauze, tulle and satin were taken home to the fine ladies; to-day very likely they are all faded, soiled and torn—but that is nothing to me—the important thing is that they are finished, and that my mistress had time to look at her workwomen. I looked so badly, that she asked me if I was ill. I could not help crying, and I told her that unfortunately it was not I who was ill, but my father and mother. She asked me why I had not remained at home and taken care of them. I told her all—and here is a little paper that she gave me, that mamma might know that I had permission to stay with her. And now let us have our supper, my good little Jean Paul; I have only bought some bread, because, you see——"

"Oh!" said Jean Paul, interrupting her, "bread is so good!"

He would have liked the bread very much, and something besides to eat with it; but he knew why Madeleine had not bought more, and he did not want to distress her. He asked her, however, if she knew where her mother had put his two francs.

Madeleine did not know, and she begged him not to ask her mother.

"Mamma would be too much worried, if she knew that we had not any money. Wait until she is stronger, before we tell her."

CHAPTER XII

The little tickets

MME. BIENFAIT passed a good night. It had struck eleven o'clock in the morning, and Jean Paul had not come in to see his neighbor. Suddenly, Madeleine heard a great noise of something falling in the entry. Mme. Bienfait, who was dozing, woke up, and asked what was the matter. Madeleine opened the door, and saw our friend Jean Paul lying on the floor under a heap of sticks of wood, some of which were rolling along the entry.

"Come and help me, Madeleine," cried he. "Come and pick up this big stick of wood, which is going to fall down the staircase. Then the bread. Take care of the cheese!"

"My lady and Rosette are not hurt, I hope?"

"No, they are in my pocket."

"Let us know, Jean Paul; come in and tell us why you are loaded in this way like a donkey."

"First, then, as you did not want me, I have been out since early this morning with my ladies the mice, who began to be tired at being shut up so long. We have made a few sous. Then I went to the baker's, and bought this big piece of bread that you see. I then saw a very nice little roll, and I asked the baker's wife, who is a very pleasant woman, how much a little roll like that would cost. 'You mustn't ask too much for it,' I said to her; 'it is for a person sick in bed, and who has not eaten anything for four days; a little white

roll like that must be good, isn't it?' In the shop there
was a lady who had just done something with some
little pieces of pasteboard that she was counting. 'My
little man,' said she to me, 'if your invalid has been ill
four days, it is not bread that she wants, it is soup.'
'Oh yes, I know that,' I said, 'but soup is——' I think
I turned very red. 'It is very dear, isn't it? And that
is why you didn't think of it.' I made a motion that it
was so. Then she felt in her pocket, and took out of
it a small bundle of little cards of different colors. She
chose a red one, and said to me, 'Look here, they will
give for this enough meat to make a little soup for
your invalid.' Then she added, 'You must have fire
to make soup.' Then she gave me a little green ticket,
and said, 'That is for the wood.' Then she left without
giving me time to thank her. I did not understand it
at all. I turned my tickets over and over again in my
hands, without knowing what to do with them. The
baker's wife had pity on me; she explained that I must
go with my little green card to the wood dealer, and
with my little red ticket to the butcher; that one would
give me wood, the other meat. I have been to the wood
dealer, and here is the wood. Hurrah! But I wanted
to show you how funny these little tickets are, so I
brought you the red one."

"Look!" said Madeleine; "there is writing on it."

Madeleine took it, and read slowly, "In the name of
our Lord Jesus Christ (Oh that ought to be good if it
comes from the sweet Jesus). In the name of our
Lord Jesus Christ. Good for two pounds of beef to
be had of——, butcher, —— street, &c."

"The signature I cannot read."

"It must be the name of the clergyman of our parish," said Mme. Bienfait, in a weak voice. "That is what they call a meat ticket. I do believe a little soup would do me good, my child. Take the ticket, and go and get a piece of meat."

Jean Paul went out with Madeleine. As soon as they were in the entry, he said to her,

"You know that I am going to stay with your mother to-day; I will bring the meat, and make the soup. Don't be worried, I know how—my mother taught me how to make soup."

"But why can't I stay, too?" said Madeleine.

"Because it is Thursday," said Jean Paul. "Did you not say that on Thursday the relatives of the sick people at the hospital could go and see them? And your father, Madeleine!"

"It is true," said the poor child. "It is Thursday! And that I should forget it! I have been so unhappy all this week, that I did not know what day it was. My poor father would be most unhappy if I did not go to see him. O my good Jean Paul, I may say to him, that mamma is much better, almost well, mayn't I?"

"Certainly," said our little friend. "When you return, and after she has taken some of this good soup, we can help her up, and make her bed. You will see!"

"Good-bye, and thank you, dear Jean Paul," said Madeleine. "I will go as fast as possible, that I may come back sooner."

But she had not gone three steps before she returned to Jean Paul.

"Poor little Jean Paul! you only think of us, my father and my mother, and you do not think of your-

self. See what fine weather it is to-day! You will
lose the whole afternoon in taking care of mamma."

Jean Paul interrupted her:

"Ah well! is this the way you hurry? Go quickly,
and let me go to the butcher's; your mother is waiting
for her soup."

Madeleine ran off as fast as she could, and he went
to the butcher's.

When Madeleine came back, Mme. Bienfait was
seated at the corner of the fire, in her old armchair, and
with her feet on a footstool. Madeleine screamed with
joy.

"Father is up too!" she cried. She threw her arms
around her mother, and kissed her again and again
with great tenderness. "Dear father and mother are
almost cured! Oh! I thank Thee dear God!" said she,
getting up again, her face beaming with joy. Then
she saw her little friend half hid under a big mattress
which he was trying to turn over.

"Well, idler that I am, in my joy I have let you make
the bed alone. Wait, I'll help you, and you shall see
if I have any strength."

They were a long time making the bed, the children
were so gay. They made up by their laughter for their
many days of sadness. The mattress, the sheets, the
covering, the pillows flew like balloons from one to the
other. At last, in spite of all this, the bed was made,
and well made too, as the invalid slept well in it. Before she went to bed she insisted upon Madeleine and
Jean Paul eating a little soup and meat. They would
not touch the precious soup that the invalid needed;
Jean Paul even regretted taking a little piece of beef.

Chapter XIII

Rain and tears

T HE next day and the following ones, Jean Paul went out early and came home late. In the morning before starting, and in the evening when he came back, he knocked at Mme. Bienfait's door.

"Are all well?" cried he.

"Yes!" answered Madeleine, "wait a minute; I will open the door."

"No! no!" said Jean Paul, "I am in too great a hurry."

"We never see him now," said Mme. Bienfait, "the good little fellow who tended me so faithfully!"

"He knows we do not need him now, and he is trying to earn a few sous," the little girl answered.

If Madeleine had followed our friend, she would have seen him stop very often, without doing anything, under the porte-cochères where he sheltered himself when it rained, or when he was tired. She did not suspect that Jean Paul would not come in because he did not want to eat the breakfast or supper that Mme. Bienfait would be sure to offer him. He knew that the money drawer was empty, and that sickness had not made it any fuller.

However, one morning, he went into his friend's room. My lady and Rosette were on his shoulder in full dress; he came to ask the way to the Champs Elysées which Madeleine had so often spoken of to him. He could earn nothing more in that neighborhood; everybody had seen the little animals, and scarcely any one even looked at them now.

"But," said Madeleine, "do you know that it is very far off?"

"For that reason I intend to start early, as you see," answered Jean Paul.

"Do you think we shall have fine weather? It has rained so hard these last few days," she added.

"Oh! there's the sun!" said Jean Paul; "and if it

should rain, I will go under shelter and wait. Tell me at once, Madeleine."

"Well," replied she, "you must go to the river; you know the way there?"

Jean Paul nodded an affirmative.

"When you reach the wharf, you must turn to the left, and then you must go alongside of the river, ever so far—and then, mamma?"

"Afterwards," said Mme. Bienfait, "you will see some large trees on the opposite side of the river; and then you will have to cross the bridge. Start off, my boy; you will do better to ask your way there. Madeleine, is there not something to eat that you can give to the poor child, who is going so far?"

"Thank you, thank you, my good lady," said Jean Paul, shutting the door, and running off as fast as his legs could carry him.

When he went out of the house he stopped a moment to think, and then started on the route that his little friend had pointed out to him. He reached the wharf very easily, and went slowly along the bank of the river. While walking along, he looked at the running water. He had heard, as all children have, that little streams make big rivers, and he asked himself, he who knew nothing of geography, if the torrents from his dear mountains and the clear stream where his mother washed his clothes, met here, and were running before him; and then his thoughts went back to the little house at Escaladios.

He bore the walk very well, and fortunately, also, the way was straight. Hours passed on—all at once however our friend felt very tired. His thoughts came

back to Paris. He was still on the wharf, and the river
ran beneath him. Opposite to him, beyond the water,
he saw a large number of leafless trees and there was
a bridge lower down. That must be the one that
Mme. Bienfait told him of— "I must be quiet near
the Champs Elysées."

Just then a porter passed by him, and he asked him.
Yes, that was the Champs Elysées, a little way to the
right, and then to the left. He only had to cross the
bridge, and the Place de la Concorde, that great square
full of statues.

Jean Paul felt quite encouraged. He took a piece of
bread from his pocket, and began to jump and sing
while he was eating it, and now he has reached the
bridge and is on it. It is pleasant to cross a bridge on
a fine river that is always running. How fast the
pieces of wood, and everything that is on it, go! The
bridge itself is immovable. But what was this Jean
Paul felt on his hand! He lifted his nose in the air,
and down came two drops, ten drops, a hundred drops.
It has begun to rain, and is raining very hard.

"Quick! my ladies, go into my pocket!" said Jean
Paul, "and let us run and find a shelter."

Indeed, he starts off as fast as his legs can carry
him. The rain increases, he is blinded with it; but he
runs straight on, avoiding the carriages which crossed
each other in every direction. He thought he saw some
houses near him on the right. But when he got there,
and looked for a door, there was none. He went on and
on, he passed the wall, and there was a great iron gate
opening into a garden. Poor Jean Paul! It was the
wall and the gate of the garden of the Tuileries. He

was now wet to the skin, and water ran from his cap into his eyes, his hair was plastered on his face and neck. He hurried on still faster. At last there were houses and a real door, where a great many people were sheltering themselves. But the sky began to clear. The rain was over. Jean Paul brushed the hair from his eyes, and shook himself a little. Then all at once he thought of the mice. He put his hand quickly into his pocket, and took it away horrified. "They are wet! so wet, so wet!" said he.

Then he went into the hospitable door; every one had left the shelter, and he seated himself on a little step, and took from his pocket—what? Two little animals with green noses, green feet, and green tails; both clothed in green rags all tumbled, and disgusting with green water.

Jean Paul understood how it was; my lady's dress had dyed Rosette's apron, hat, nose, feet and tail, and as for his bread, which he had put in his pocket when the rain began, it was quite green. Jean Paul did not speak, or cry; he was completely overwhelmed, and he stood there without moving.

Suddenly he heard the cry of "Clear the way there!" which made him start. It was a carriage that was driving into the yard. Jean Paul jumped aside quickly that he might not be crushed, and he put his poor little mice, mechanically, in his waistcoat pocket. He left the house; he did not know where to go. Still, mechanically he asked some one the way to the Champs Elysées. "The Champs Elysées," he thought, "why should I go there? Who would give a pin now to see my lady and Rosette? My poor little mice, that I loved so much! It was you, my dear mother, who made their pretty clothes! You did not want me to start, you were right; I have nothing now by which I can gain my livelihood. What will become of me?"

Our poor friend went back hardly knowing what he was doing. He again crossed the Place de la Concorde and the bridge, and walked along the wharves slowly and sadly. He looked at nothing; neither saw, felt nor thought of anything. Soon the sun, which had shown itself, disappeared, and the rain came down hard and heavy. In a minute the wharves were deserted—all the people ran to shelter themselves. Jean Paul alone went on his way without hurrying himself. He was indifferent to everything; he was so unhappy.

The rain poured in torrents when he reached the old house. He passed slowly before the lodge and went up the narrow staircase, when he heard some one call him by name. He turned back and went into the yard again. M. Fumeron had half opened his lodge window.

"Tell me, Jean Paul," he said, "do you know that the water-carriers come before eleven o'clock in the morning and it is now four o'clock in the afternoon? I will make you pay a fine. Hi, hi, hi!" he laughed, "you are carrying at least a bucket of water in your trousers and as much in your vest. Hi, hi, hi! you will flood all the house! Hi, hi! it is not allowed."

He shut the window, and Jean Paul heard his silly wicked laugh, which continued until a violent fit of coughing put a stop to it. Our friend remained in the rain while listening to him; he made him no answer. He crossed the yard, and went up the staircase slowly and sadly.

He arrived at last at his room, took out the key, shut the door, and threw himself full length on his bundle of straw. This did not please my ladies the mice, for they found themselves so smothered by the weight of Jean Paul's body that they began to scratch with their eight feet, and to utter such piercing cries, that he put his hand in his bosom, took them both out at once, and put them on the ground, without looking at them. Then he crossed his arms over his head. What could he do, poor child? He wept, and wept violently.

At nightfall, a light step was heard in the entry. It was Madeleine. She went into her mother's room. A minute after, she knocked at Jean Paul's door. There was no answer.

"He has not come in yet, my good mother; you were mistaken," she said with her sweet voice.

"I am sure I heard him, however," said Mme. Bienfait.

It was ten o'clock; by degrees, all the lights in the house were put out. Madeleine opened her chamber door, and knocked again at Jean Paul's door. She knocked loudly, and called him. Not a word in reply. Jean Paul did not move. "Oh, he can not have come in," said she to her mother, "he must have lost his way in his long walk."

"Be calm, my child," said Mme. Bienfait, "this poor little boy has already taken a great many long walks. Only think of it, he has walked alone all through France."

"That is true!" but nevertheless she sighed.

Soon after, the light was put out in Mme. Bienfait's room also.

In the middle of the night Madeleine woke up suddenly. A light was shining in her eyes. She started, and sat up in her bed. What was it she saw? Her mother, who had got up tottering, and was putting on her petticoat and slippers, had taken the candle and was about leaving the room.

"Why did you get up, mamma, when you are so weak, and still cough so much?" cried Madeleine, who leaped from her bed, and ran to her mother to take her back again.

"Go to bed at once, mother. What is the matter?"

"It is true, I have not strength enough to stand up, my child," said her mother, lying down again. "But we must see what ails the dear child."

"Why, who, mamma?"

"Listen!" said her mother. "Listen!" Madeleine listened—she heard a deep groan.

"What is that?" said she; "who is it that suffers so?"

"It can only be our little friend. I was going to see what had happened to him, when you woke up."

"I'll go, mamma, I'll go," said Madeleine, hastily putting on her dress and taking the light.

"Jean Paul! my good little Jean Paul! What is the matter with you? Are you sick or hurt? Let me in, I beg you. I beseech you to open the door. You are there; I hear you; you are crying. It was mamma who sent me—she heard you groaning all night. I will not go away until I have seen you. I would rather pass the night.at.your door."

At last Madeleine heard the rustling of the straw; the key was turned in the lock, and the door was opened. Jean Paul covered with his hand his eyes swollen by crying; he could not bear the light.

"Oh, dear me!" said Madeleine, taking her friend's arm, "how wet you are! you are as cold as ice; how you tremble! What has happened, Jean Paul? You are going to be ill, that is certain."

"That would be nothing," said Jean Paul in a low voice, "but look, there is the great misfortune, look."

He pointed with his finger to a little shapeless heap in the corner. Madeline stooped down, and held the candle near to see better.

"Oh," said she, "it is my lady and Rosette! What a misfortune!"

She stood there overwhelmed.

"Take care of the candle! Do not set fire to the straw!" cried Mme. Bienfait from her bed.

"Oh, that is true! the fire!" said Madeleine. "I did not think of it."

She picked up the candle again, which she had put upon the floor; and taking hold of Jean Paul's hand firmly, drew him by force into her mother's room.

"Look, mamma," said she on coming in, "look at him, wet to the skin, and cold and trembling; and the worst of it is, that his mice are in the same plight."

She could not restrain her tears, and began to sob.

"Let us see," said Mme. Bienfait. "But try not to cry, dear little one."

She took Jean Paul by the hand.

"First of all, we must warm him; light the fire, Madeleine; see how his teeth chatter. Put the coffee-pot upon the coals, that he may have something warm to drink. I do not want you to be ill, as I have been, my dear boy. But you must really change your clothes. Have you any other clothes than these, my little friend?"

Jean Paul said, "No."

"Let me see," she said, "how can we manage it? We must not leave these wet clothes on him. My husband's are three times too big for him. Oh, I see now, get that little black wadded petticoat out of the wardrobe, and then give him one of your chemises, and your little blue saque. Now, my dear child, go into your room, take off your wet clothes; put these on; and above all, come back quickly. Take the candle—the fire gives us plenty of light; and do not go near the straw with it."

Jean Paul did as he was told. When he came back, dressed in Madeleine's blue saque, and Mme. Bienfait's black petticoat, which trailed on the ground, Madeleine, in spite of her sadness was seized with a fit of laughing, and Mme. Bienfait would have joined in, if she had not seen Jean Paul's sad face.

"Come to the fire," she said to him; "you feel better already, don't you?"

"No," answered Jean Paul by a motion of his head.

"What! no? Do you suffer more?"

"Oh no, it is nothing," he said at last; "but the poor little creatures!"

"Go, bring them here, Jean Paul," said Madeleine, "so that we may warm the unfortunate little things."

When Jean Paul came back holding in his hand something green which moved, Madeleine began to cry and lament.

In the meantime Mme. Bienfait was examining my ladies the mice.

"Why, they are not dead at all," said she. "If these wet rags were taken off of them, they would be as lively as usual."

"I know very well that they are not dead," said Jean Paul, "but it is the same as if they were, now that they have neither dresses nor hats, nor anything to be dressed with. Their white hair is even all spoiled."

"If you are only crying for their dresses, and the whiteness of their skin, it will be all right," said Mme. Bienfait, laughing. "As for their dresses, I will make them."

"You, madame? Do you know how to work like mother?" said Jean Paul, holding his head up and beginning to smile.

"Yes, yes, my friend, I have been sewing twenty-five years. I have made dresses for greater ladies than Lady Green Satin."

"And do you know how to make an apron, and a hat?"

"An apron, a hat, two hats—all that you want."

"Oh! what—"

Jean Paul did not finish, but again looked very sad.

"But with those ugly green noses nothing will look well."

"Oh, it is very easy to change that," said Madame Bienfait, laughing. "Madeleine, give me a little warm water and soap. Undress the mice, Jean Paul. Now rub their skin softly with soap; a drop of water. Rub well, that's it! There they are whiter than ever! And now, my boy, come to the fire, warm yourself, and then go to bed."

Jean Paul was radiant with joy. He took a chair and seated himself in front of the fire, holding his dear little mice on his knees near it, to dry them better.

"You seem as if you were trembling yet, Jean Paul," said Madeleine, "are you still cold, by this good fire?"

"Oh, I am too happy to feel cold," said our friend, whose teeth still chattered. "I am very warm, thank you!"

"Give him some wine immediately, Madeleine; that will do him good."

"That is true," said Madeleine, running towards the cupboard. "Here, Jean Paul, uncork this bottle, you are stronger than I am. Do not say no. Do not be so ceremonious. Mother insists upon your drinking it, and I also. Come! pull hard, pull hard! You seem to be astonished that we have good wine here, and fire, and wood, and bread!" (She opened the drawer and showed Jean Paul a five-franc piece and some change.) "You must know that to-day I went to see my father; he is much better. In a few days he will come back again." (She jumped with joy.) "He asked me what money we had in the house, and when I told him we had none, he wrote a few lines with a pencil, and told me to carry it to his employer, who owed him money. His employer gave me ten francs. You must know," said she, "that my father is a working lock-smith; he is more than a workman, he is the same as master—but is not quite master yet."

"Your father is foreman," interrupted Mme. Bienfait. "Now, Madeleine, stop chattering, this minute. Pour out some wine in the glass. And you, my little friend, drink it quickly. There, now you feel better. Oh! I am sure that you are hungry. Madeleine, give him what was left from our dinner—no ceremony, my boy. Come, eat, drink, and warm yourself. When you feel quite well, you had better go to bed."

Two o'clock struck. Madeleine and Jean Paul were so busy talking, that half an hour had passed before the idea came to them that night was the time for sleeping. Jean Paul was quite gay again; his cheeks had become rosy, and his hands warm and soft; as for my ladies the mice, they would have run all over the chamber, had not their master held them fast upon his knees.

Mme. Bienfait saw all this at a glance; she put her hand upon the candlestick.

"My children, I tell you now, that I am going to count ten, and then put out the candle. Go, Jean Paul, if you want to have light to open your door and, Madeleine, do you also go to bed."

"First, I beg of you, mother, to let me say something very useful. My mistress has told me that I must begin to work again," said she to Jean Paul. "I will go there again to-morrow very early. Since you cannot go out with your mice, will you pass the day with mamma? You can run her little errands, and cook for her; she is still so weak."

"Yes, yes," answered Jean Paul.

Then the obedient child leaned over Mme. Bienfait's bed, and kissed her affectionately, and ran to his room.

How well he slept, this good little boy! The long walk of the day before, his emotion, his grief, his joy, had fatigued him so much, that he did not open his eyes until nine o'clock in the morning. He hurried to go to Mme. Bienfait. It had been an hour since Madeleine had left, delighted, she said, to hear Jean Paul snoring still.

CHAPTER XIV

'Tis an ill wind that blows no one good

THE day passed, and Mme. Bienfait to the great astonishment and even to the great grief of Jean Paul, did not seem to remember the promise she had made him the evening before. She did not appear to know even that there lived in the world a Lady Green Satin and her maid Rosette.

In the afternoon, Jean Paul asked permission to leave her for a moment, in order to feed his poor little animals, he said.

He emphasized very much the words "poor little

animals;" and turned quite red, fearing that Mme.
Bienfait might suspect his intention. But Mme. Bienfait did not remark it.

"Go, my child," said she; "I do not need you now."

It was night; Jean Paul lighted the candle and seated
himself at the fireside.

Some one opened the door. It was Madeleine.

"For you, Jean Paul," she said, and she threw at
his head a little bundle wrapped up in newspaper.

The bundle fell on the ground; Madeleine ran and
picked it up and threw it again to Jean Paul, saying to
him:

"No, it is not for you; it is for them."

Jean Paul caught hold of it this time. He brought
it to the light, opened it. Oh, joy! In it there were
beautiful pieces of silk, of gauze, and of velvet, ends of
ribbon, black and white lace, and trimmings of gold
and silver braid.

Jean Paul understood it in a moment. He threw
his arms around Mme. Bienfait's neck.

"And I thought you had forgotten them!" said he.

"I saw that very plainly, my child, but I could not
tell you; I had promised Madeleine that she should have
the pleasure of surprising you."

"It was all arranged this morning," said Madeleine.

"How beautiful they are!" said Jean Paul, touching
the pretty stuffs with the end of his finger; "what magnificent little dresses they will make!"

"Indeed, they are very pretty," said Madeleine quick-
ly. "My mistress works for the most elegant ladies.
Look, this blue velvet is a piece of the dress of the
Duchess Batti. But what is that to us? The best of

all is, that my mistress has given me permission to stay
at home to-morrow and work with you, mamma.   I
told her you had some work which must be finished;
I did not tell a story, did I, mamma?"

"Ask Jean Paul if he is in a hurry to see my lady
dressed," answered Mme. Bienfait, laughing.

"Oh! I am in a very great hurry," said Jean Paul.

"I was thinking to-day," Madeleine said suddenly,
"how you were able to bring my lady and Rosette from
the Pyrenees to Paris without their being wet with the
rain."

"They were often a little so in their cage, but their
dresses were safe in a little box.   They did not wear
them excepting on Sundays and fine days."

"Then why don't you carry the little box with you
when you go out here?" said Madeleine.

"Oh! in Paris there are porte-cochères, so that when
it rains I can get shelter," replied Jean Paul.

"Yes," said Madeleine, "excepting on bridges and
in squares."

Jean Paul said firmly, "When I go to the Champs
Elysées again I will go by some other way, so that I
will not have to cross the river."

Mme. Bienfait and Madeleine burst out laughing.

"I wish you may find such a way!" said Madeleine.
"The river divides Paris into two parts, my child," said
Mme. Bienfait.   "If you want to go to the Tuileries or
Champs Elysées, you will have to cross the bridge."

Jean Paul sighed deeply and did not answer.

"An idea strikes me!" said Madeleine suddenly.
"You shall be able to cross bridges, even when the rain
pours in torrents, if you like, and not one drop of water

can touch either my lady or Rosette—and their umbrella will not be heavy to carry, either."

She opened the lower drawer of the bureau and took
out of it a large bundle of oiled silk.

"You know, mamma," said she, showing it to her
mother, "this was given to my father for his rheumatism, but he could not use it. Let me make a little bag
like those we saw at the hairdresser's."

"A sponge bag?" asked Mme. Bienfait.

"That's it! Only this will be a mouse bag. I will
make it rather large, with a good drawing-string on
top. Jean Paul can carry it in his pocket. If a drop
of rain falls, Jean Paul opens the bag, pops my lady
and Rosette at once into it, and that without rumpling
their dresses. Then he draws the string, passes the
cords over his arm, and walks on as if his handkerchief and purse were in the bag!"

"Hurrah! good luck!" said Jean Paul, jumping with
joy.

Madeleine did the same; and it was at least five
minutes before Mme. Bienfait could make herself
heard.

"It is not a bad idea, little one," said she, "only if
Jean Paul draws the strings of his bag too tight, he
will find my lady and Rosette suffocated when he wants
to take them out."

"I shall find them suf— what, madam, please?" said
Jean Paul, with open mouth.

"Suffocated, my child; that is to say, dead for want
of air to breathe. No man, no animal, no matter how
small it may be, can live without air. But don't be
uneasy; I will take care that Madeleine makes little

windows at the top of the bag, so the dear little creatures will not be in any danger."

"Mamma, will you let me make the little bag this evening? It will amuse me so much! You do not like me to sit up, I know; but I assure you I am not at all tired to-day."

Mme. Bienfait consented. Madeleine took her measures, cut, shaped, clipped, and finished the bag that evening, with its drawing-string and its little windows.

As soon as the beds were made the next day, the floor swept, and the furniture carefully dusted, Madeleine and her mother began to work.

It was two o'clock; the sun shone through the window, and, falling upon the worktable, made the little pieces of silk and velvet that covered it look quite brilliant. Madeleine held in her hand a little skirt of red moiré silk, and Mme. Bienfait has something so very small in hers that it must be a hat.

"Mamma," said Madeleine, standing the skirt on the table, and turning it on all sides in order to admire it the more, "are you sure that the table will be large enough?"

"What table?" asked Mme. Bienfait, putting down her work also, and leaning her tired back against the chair.

"This, I mean," said the child, giving a little knock of her hand on the worktable.

"Big enough for what? Explain yourself, my dear."

"Why, mamma, our Sunday dinner. You know that father is coming home on Saturday, and that on Sunday we are to have a tablecloth and are going to give a grand dinner to dear father and to Jean Paul. There must be a jubilee now that both my dear parents are cured. Jean Paul and my father must become acquainted also, dear mamma, mustn't they?"

"Poor Jean Paul!" sighed Mme. Bienfait.

"Why do you pity him, mamma? Is he so much poorer than we are? He is well, he is gay."

"It is true that we are poor, my dear," interrupted Mme. Bienfait, "almost as poor as he; yet I am sure your father would not like to sit down beside him at table."

"You think so, mamma! is it possible? And father is so good!"

"But our poor Jean Paul is so dirty! Have you not noticed, Madeleine, his yellow face, his hair like brushwood, his black hands, and his soiled shirt?"

"I tried not to see all that," said Madeleine, timidly.

"Yes, but your father will see it at once. You know how fond he is of cleanliness, and with what care every morning and evening, and indeed many times a day, he washes his face and hands and combs his hair."

"O mamma, Jean Paul is so poor! It is not his fault that he is so dirty."

"You are wrong, my dear; it is not necessary to have money to be clean: it is courage that is wanted. In winter there are rich people who, in their warm rooms, are too cowardly to put a drop of water on their skin."

"That is true," interrupted Madeleine. "My mistress told us the other day of a lady who came to try on a splendid velvet dress, and whose neck and arms were quite soiled."

"You see, then, my dear, that it only requires courage to wash oneself."

Madeleine thought a moment.

"Now, for once, it is I who am right, mamma!" cried she. "Jean Paul has but one shirt—he told me so. How can he change it, then?"

"If he were very courageous and very cleanly," said Mme. Bienfait, laughing, "he would have done as others have done; he might have gone without a shirt, and taken his to the washhouse, and put it on again when it was dry." She added, sighing, "What! this unfortunate child has but one shirt! But now I think of it, I have an old shirt of your father's—I can cut it up, take away the wornout part, and it will make an excellent one for our friend. I will let you finish the dresses for the mice, my dear; besides, my poor eyes are tired and I shall do better on coarser work."

"I shall be very much pleased to see him in a white shirt," said Madeleine, while her mother cut the coarse linen.

"I am afraid his face and hands will only appear more dirty," answered Mme. Bienfait.

"Oh!" said Madeleine, laughing, "he took a rain-bath yesterday, at the same time that his mice did. That's something gained. 'It's an ill wind that blows no one good.'" Then she added more seriously, "What is to be done to teach him to be cleanly? I dare not tell him that my father—well, yes, I will do it. Poor Jean Paul! ——Mamma," said she after a moment's silence, "is it very wicked to be dirty?"

"Ask your conscience, dear little one. It will tell you that dirtiness is not a vice, like lying or anger, but that at the same time it cannot be pleasing to God, since it makes us disagreeable to those about us.   And then uncleanliness is the daughter of idleness, and cleanliness is said to be next to godliness."

Just then some one knocked at the door, and Jean Paul's voice asked,

"May I come in, good Madame Bienfait?"

Madeleine's mother put her finger to her lips anu said, in a low voice,

"Do not speak of it now."

Madeleine made a gesture of obedience.

"I have but a stitch more to do," cried she to Jean Paul.

Since the morning the workers had not allowed Jean Paul to come into the room.   Madeleine wanted to have the costumes completely finished before Jean Paul saw them.

She at last broke off the silken thread with which she was sewing, cleared the table of the scraps, and carefully placed there, first the superb dress, with a train of cherry-colored moiré antique, then the little saque of the same, and a hat of black velvet trimmed with gold.

"That is for my lady!" said she.

A little further off, she put delicately upon the table a skirt of blue taffeta, turned up over a little petticoat striped with gold and blue, a little body of black velvet, and a darling little lace hat trimmed with blue ribbon. And this was for Rosette!

"Now you can come in, Monsieur Jean Paul," said she.

"Well!" said she, as soon as he had opened the door, "have your seamstresses worked well?"

"Oh!—ah!—oh!—ah!" cried Jean Paul, wonder-stricken with what he saw on the table. "Oh!!"——he wished to speak, but joy and admiration hindered the words from coming.

"If we light the lamp, mamma! It is dusk now, he can't see the things well."

"Oh! yes I can, my good Madeleine! How beautiful they are! How good you are, Madame Bienfait! And this skirt is so rich that it stands alone! Oh! there, there! I would like to be a mouse to wear these beau-tiful dresses! Oh! and this little hat! and this little saque, with these long strings hanging from the back!"

"Those strings are called, 'Follow me, young man,'" said Madeleine, "the last fashion!"

"This will bring them good luck. I am very sure that they will be so handsome, both old and young will follow them."

"Go, bring the little creatures," said Madeleine; "I want to try their dresses on. I hope these ladies will be pleased with their mantua-makers," said she, making a little curtsey and throwing down her eyes.

Jean Paul went away backwards, not to lose sight of the things that were on the table, and continued his "ah's" and "oh's." He was speechless with delight.

"You will die with joy when I tell you that I have not used half of my scraps, and mamma and I want to make two more costumes for your mice."

Jean Paul remained motionless, as if petrified with pleasure.

"Go and get them," repeated Madeleine after a moment, bursting out laughing and pushing him towards the door. "I thought that you were gone."

"Oh! mamma, how happy it makes one to give so much joy to another!" said Madeleine, leaning towards her mother to kiss her. "It seems to me it will be like this in heaven, and we shall be happy in seeing those happy who surround us."

Mme. Bienfait put down her work and pressed her daughter in her arms.

Jean Paul returned, bringing the mice. My good lady was a little sleepy and did not seem inclined to be dressed, nor Rosette, either. However, they allowed themselves to be dressed and admired with a very good grace. Jean Paul, in order to show his gratitude to Madeleine, wanted to have a performance; but these ladies, a little frightened by the light of the lamp, and not quite at ease in their new dresses, would not stand up, but fell down on their four feet just as common mice. Jean Paul scolded, and Madeleine laughed with all her heart.

"You were right to thank us yourself, my dear boy," said Mme. Bienfait, "for I think that if the mice knew how to speak, they would not thank us at all. They were enchanted, I know, to have no other clothing than their white fur for the last few days."

"They must not learn bad habits," said Jean Paul seriously.

Our good little friend did not allow himself to be discouraged. By scolding and caressing them by turns, by scolding them again, and sundry little taps on the back, he succeeded at last in making them play and showing all their pretty little tricks.

Mme. Bienfait, Madeleine and Jean Paul all three declared that the new dresses were still finer than the old ones. After the performance they were carefully taken off and folded up.

Madeleine wanted to change the names of these interesting little animals, and call them Lady Red Moiré

and Bluette. But after a long discussion it was decided they should keep the famous names of Lady Green Satin and Rosette, "already well known through the world," said Jean Paul.

They embraced each other very affectionately. Jean Paul thanked them again and then went to his room. In his prayer that night he returned thanks to God for having given him such good friends and asked Him to bless them.

Chapter XV

A cat!

IT was four o clock in the morning; it was dark, very
dark. Everybody was asleep. Jean Paul opened
his eyes—he had heard a noise. He was still sleepy
and he fell asleep.

He woke again. Some one, or something, was moving the straw on which he slept. It made a great noise
in the deep silence of the night.

And then something heavy fell upon him, which with
a bound, jumped, and fell on the floor. Jean Paul
raised his head from the straw, then he sat up, he listened, his heart beat. There was something in the
room, which came and went, which ran and stopped,
and jumped. Jean Paul had just seen two big eyes,
shining like coals. They are not the little eyes of my
lady and Rosette.

"Horrible!" cried he. "It is the cat!" He raised
himself suddenly, and threw himself upon the animal.
He caught it easily; his chamber was so small. He carried it in his arms, half opened the door, put it outside,
and shut it quickly.

"It is Madame Fumeron's cat, Minet; it must have
followed me yesterday; if only it has done no harm to
my lady and Rosette!" thought he. He did not dare
to say, "If only it has not eaten them!"

118

He called "Mini! Little ones, little ones! Mini!" as he did usually. There was no answer.

"They are still afraid of the cat," said he, "they have crept into some corner. I ought always to shut them up in their travelling cage. But the dear little ones love their liberty so much it seems cruel to confine them. Oh, I wish it were day!"

He turned to go to bed, when he put his foot on something soft and warm. He started back hastily, and then got down on his hands and knees and felt for it with his hands.

He found it, he picked it up, he felt it with care; it was quite small and covered with fine hair. Jean Paul felt the little feet, the long slender tail, the two tiny ears, the pointed nose; it was—it was a mouse! A mouse that the cat had killed and was going to eat. The unfortunate child covered it with kisses and tears.

"Poor little thing!" said he sobbing, "and I to be sleeping! How wicked I was not to have known how to save them!"

"Which one is it?" said he suddenly.

"Ah! it is my lady. I know her by her size! No, it is Rosette! My lady's tail is not so long! Poor Rosette!" He began kissing her again. "But no, it is my lady, which is still more unlucky."

He took the little dead animal so near the window that its fur touched the glass; but it was all in vain, not a ray of light; still dark night.

"And your companion, poor little thing! Where is she? Eaten, devoured by that frightful beast!"

Just then Jean Paul thought he heard a little scratching in the straw which he used as a bed. He held his breath; he listened, he listened again; another scratching, then a little cry, *"He! he! he!"*

"One is alive yet!" cried he. "Which one? Which one? Oh, how I wish it were day!"

It was not very warm in our friend's room at night; he lay down in his straw, still holding his dear little animal in his hand and listening to the faint noise of the one who had escaped death.

His eyes were wide open; he thought of the pretty clothes which had become useless, of the grief of Madeleine, and then of his poor mother, who would never again receive any money from her Jean Paul; it was all over. He cried all the time; he could not console himself. After a while his eyes closed, but he would have liked better to have remained awake. He dreamt that he was giving a great performance in the garden of the Tuileries. A crowd of children surrounded him. The mice, in their new dresses, showed their backs to the public. They turned around. Oh! what a misfortune! there was nothing in their dresses or hats, the hats and dresses were empty!

"Jean Paul, you know very well that it was the cat that ate them," said a little fair girl.

Jean Paul awoke suddenly; he was wet with perspiration. But he still held tightly clasped in his hand the little dead animal. And now the day began to dawn; the first thing he looked at was the mouse. Is he still dreaming? No, he is wide awake. The little light which came through the window fell on the mouse which he held so carefully in his hand, and he saw that it was a gray mouse, quite gray, and of the prettiest gray! What joy! what happiness! And he still heard the same scratching underneath his bed.

He jumped up like a crazy person, took up the straw in his arms, and found close to each other, trembling, but still alive, my lady and Rosette, who, to escape from their enemy, had buried themselves in the furthest corner of the straw.

The terrible cat continued mewing in the entry, and the poor little creatures listened with terror.

Jean Paul took them in his hands and kissed them.

"So you have friends who come to see you, you little rogues!" said he to them, while showing them the poor gray mouse. Then he prudently shut them up in their old cage, opened the door of his room and drove away the cat.

"A cat, a cat!" cried he, stamping with his foot in the entry.

He still held the dead mouse in his hand. Suddenly he threw it to Minet.

"Now that it is dead," said he, "as soon as she has eaten it she will be satisfied."

The cat ran off with its prey.

Jean Paul rushed to Mme. Bienfait's door.

"Saved, saved!" said he. "Do not be afraid!"

"Bless me! what is the matter?" cried Mme. Bienfait, waking up suddenly. "What do you want, my child? What is the matter? I am coming!"

"No, no," cried Jean Paul, "stay where you are. They are saved."

"Saved, who?" cried Mme. Bienfait.

"My lady and Rosette! the cat is gone!"

"What cat? what? Are you crazy, my child?" asked

Mme. Bienfait.   "It is scarcely day, and it is biting cold; go to bed again."

"I am going, I am going, my good Madame Bienfait, I thank you; it is because I am so happy!"

He jumped for joy, then came back again.

"Saved, saved!" said he to Madeleine.   "Isn't it so?"

Madeleine slept quietly, and her mother took good care not to wake her up.

The next day all was explained; Madeleine turned pale with fear when Jean Paul told her of the danger his dear mice had been in, and good Mme. Bienfait easily pardoned our friend for having wakened her so suddenly.   As soon as Jean Paul had finished telling the history of the night he began it again, he was still so much agitated by it.   Madeleine would in the end have been tired of hearing it; but at eight o'clock she went to her mistress's and did not return until evening, as usual.

"At last!" she said, when she came in.   "To-morrow is mid-Lent! And this evening, Jean Paul, the moon shines so brightly that we shall certainly have a fine day to-morrow.   If it should be fine weather all Paris will be in the streets.   The mice have magnificent dresses; we shall do a good business, you will see.   You know, mamma, you promised me a long time ago that you would let me go out with Jean Paul at mid-Lent if it were fine weather.   You are quite well now; you will not want me."

"No, my dear, go take a walk; go with your friend, and may God open all the hearts and all the purses of those you meet, my children."

And she took them both in her arms and kissed them.

Chapter XVI

Jean Paul acquires a love for cleanliness

THE next day the sky was clear, the weather mild, and there was no mud upon the pavements. How happy Jean Paul and Madeleine were while walking through the streets filled with people. The prayer of the good mother was granted; hearts and purses were both open, and when at six o'clock in the evening they thought of returning home, Jean Paul found that he had made eighteen silver pieces and as many sous. Madeleine was pensive—almost sad. Her gaiety had left her entirely. She walked silently by the side of Jean Paul.

"Jean Paul," said she suddenly to him, "have you not noticed how rough I am?"

Madeleine had to repeat the question twice; Jean Paul thought he had not understood.

"You, Madeleine! you rough! you who are gentleness itself, a lamb! Your mother always says so, you know."

"Ah, that's true," said Madeleine, "mamma says I am gentle."

She seemed quite disappointed.

"But," she added, "you've noticed that I am lazy?"

"No, Madeleine, I've always seen you work willingly. Besides, I love you as you are. Do you know, Madeleine," he said gaily, "that I believe we have made a great deal of money to-day!"

"But," said Madeleine, without answering him, "tell me what is my greatest fault."

"I assure you, I don't know any."

"Yes, yes, I want you to think, and to try to tell me what it is!" repeated Madeleine.

"But," began Jean Paul, "I have told you already that I love you dearly; we do not see faults in those we love, you know. Tell me, dear Madeleine, how much do you think we have made to-day?"

"Well, you don't ask me what your faults are," said Madeleine, ready to cry; "I beg you to tell me mine, and I'll tell you yours."

The poor little girl had fully intended not to let the day pass without letting Jean Paul know how necessary it was to be clean. After having reflected a long time on what she should do, she thought it would be a good plan to accuse herself, before accusing her friend.

"When he shall have said that I am rough and lazy, I can tell him, without giving him so much pain, that he is not clean," she had said to herself.

But nothing succeeded. Jean Paul, instead of answering her, turned to her in a friendly way and said, "What's the matter with you, my poor Madeleine? What has troubled you? Are you tired? We have walked a great deal to-day—lean on me!"

Madeleine took Jean Paul's arm and they walked along quietly, the little girl searching her mind for some means to bring about what she had to say. All at once she began with a firm voice: "You must know, Jean Paul, that mamma, after working so diligently for your mice, is now working for you. She is making a shirt for you! Day after to-morrow my father will come home, and we are going to have our great Sunday dinner. Mamma wanted her dear little Jean Paul to look well that day. You are pleased, aren't you?"

"Your mother is always kind to me," Jean Paul replied.

"If you only knew," continued Madeleine, "that my father has always a nice white shirt on a Sunday, and that every day he combs his hair and washes his hands and face! Listen, my little Jean Paul," said Madeleine, lowering her voice, "if you want him to love you, you must do a little as he does."

Jean Paul blushed and let go Madeleine's arm.

"I see how it is," said he; "your father is a gentleman, and he will despise Jean Paul because he is poor and badly dressed."

"Yes," said Madeleine, blushing and becoming animated; "my father is a gentleman, although he is only a working locksmith.   He despises no one, but he detests dirty people."

Then she added, in a mild and caressing tone of voice, "It would be so easy for my little Jean Paul to be clean and to be loved by my father!"

She had come near him and had taken his arm again. "Let us see, Jean Paul; did you wash your face this morning?"

"No," answered Jean Paul in a low voice and with a gloomy look.

"And yesterday?"

"I do not know," said he, still in the same tone.

"And Sunday?"

"Ah! Sunday, I went to the pump in the yard, took some water in the hollow of my hand and washed my face."

"Why do you not do it every day, my dear Jean Paul?   The fountains are not made for dogs.   When my father quits the workshop in the evening he is as black as a coal.   At the first fountain he comes to he turns up his sleeves, unbuttons the collar of his shirt, then he takes a little piece of soap from his pocket, and rubs his hands, face and neck with it, until all the black coal is gone."

"But when it is cold?" said Jean Paul, shivering.

"And then poor papa is very cold, but he washes himself all the same.   Ah, little Jean Paul" (Madeleine remembered her mother's words), "we must have courage to do right, even to be clean."

Madeleine stopped; she had just noticed that she was quite alone.

Jean Paul was no longer beside her.   She looked all

around anxiously, and saw him with his head under the fountain, rubbing his face with his hands.

"Is this the way?" cried he, turning towards her, the water running from his face, which he commenced again to bathe.

"Yes, yes!" said she; "rub yourself well."

Then she went to him, took her white handkerchief from her pocket, unfolded it, and wiped her friend's head carefully.

"There!" she said; "my dear little Jean Paul, you are superb! The cold water has brought the roses to your cheeks. That does you good. You are no longer tired, are you? When you wear the white shirt that mamma has made for you, and when you blacken your shoes nicely——"

"Ah, as to my shoes," said Jean Paul, "I can do nothing with them; they are full of holes."

"More reason for cleaning them well. When a thing is worn, it looks better clean. I will lend you our brush and blacking."

Jean Paul examined himself from head to foot.

"I will brush my blouse also, and very hard, for it is very dirty."

Madeleine began to laugh.

"Brush your trowsers as much as you want to," said she; "they are woollen, and want brushing badly; your blouse is cotton; to make it clean it must be washed."

"Yes, my mother washed it every Saturday." He sighed deeply, as he always did when he spoke of his mother. "Poor mamma!" he added in a low voice.

"But," said Madeleine quickly, without noticing the sadness of her friend, "now that you are a big boy, what is to hinder you from going to the washhouse and washing your blouse yourself? You could do without it for a day. You can let a little of your gray vest be seen, which you wear underneath. I will show you where the washhouse is."

Jean Paul looked at her astonished.

"The washhouse," she said, "is a place where the workmen and workwomen go to wash their own clothes. For two sous, they give you warm and cold water. But do not be uneasy, I will explain all that you have to do. To-morrow will be Friday." (She counted on her fingers.) "You will wash your blouse in the morning— it will dry by the afternoon. I'll iron it in the evening, and you will have it Sunday, when you dine with father, or even on Saturday if you want it. My little Jean Paul will be dressed like a prince."

The two children took each other's arms and began to run; it was getting late. Madeleine's little heart was lightened of a great weight. She had given good advice to her friend, without giving him pain; Jean Paul would be clean and her father would love him.

"How happy I am! how happy!" she said in a low voice.

"How happy I am!" said Jean Paul also. "I have made a great deal of money to-day. But I am so happy! Say, Madeleine, will you answer me now? How much money do you think have we brought back to-day? I have already asked you three times, without meaning to reproach you."

But no, Madeleine did not answer; they were going in the porte-cochère of their old house and she hurried on. She crossed the court and ran up the staircase quickly, pulling her friend after her.

"Victory! mamma!" cried she, on opening her mother's door. "Look at our Jean Paul."

Mme. Bienfait started back a step on seeing our friend. She no longer saw the brown frizzled head, which looked like the brush used for removing spiders' webs from ceilings; his hair was plastered on his forehead and cheeks like a black silk cap.

"Bless me," said the good woman, "he has fallen into the river!"

"At all events, dear mother, you see that he is not drowned," said Madeleine, kissing him. "Mamma," continued she, "I bring you a rich Jean Paul, and a Jean Paul well washed and well cleaned. Victory! victory! hug him well!"

Mme. Bienfait kissed the little boy, and more willingly than she had ever done before.

"Dear child," said she, "this will not be the last time, will it? Water will become your every-day friend——"

And then, seeing that he blushed a little, she hastened to add:

"And this money? Let us see it! let us count it! Put the sous on one side, and the silver money on the other. There, my little friend."

Counting everything, Jean Paul had made twelve francs and a few sous. It was magnificent!

"With the two francs that mother has taken care of, that will make fourteen francs," said Madeleine.

"Now, how can I send this money to my mother?" said our friend. "Escaladios is so far!"

"Why, in a letter," said Mme. Bienfait.

"All that money in a letter! that will break through the paper," said Jean Paul, "and then I don't know how to write."

"You shall dictate, and I will write, poor child," answered Mme. Bienfait. "The money won't break through the paper," added she, laughing. "I know how to manage it. Bigger sums are sent by letter."

"Money is not put in a letter," said Madeleine in a low voice.

"Well, where do they put it, then?" asked our friend.

"Good night, good night," answered Madeleine; the question embarrassed her a little, and she felt tired, besides.

CHAPTER XVII

Mademoiselle Jean Paul

EARLY the next day Jean Paul knocked at his friend's door.

"What do you want?" asked the sweet voice of Madeleine.

"The shoe brush," answered Jean Paul.

"I will bring it to you," said Madeleine. "I am up; wait a minute. You see, darling mamma," said she to Mme. Bienfait, "he is quite converted. He is going to become as neat as father."

The mud was taken off the shoes in the entry; a little blacking was rubbed on very hard, and there was plenty of laughter.

When they were very shining, Jean Paul put them on and danced a mountain dance.

"We have had enough fun!" said he. "Now, little Madeleine, lend me your clothes brush. I am going into my room to take off my trowsers and brush them well."

Madeleine went into her mother's room and brought back the brush. It was a respectable brush, which by hard service had lost half its bristles.

"It is not new," said she, laughing, "but you will see that it is good. Brush them very hard, my little friend; do not leave a spot upon them; do you hear?"

As usual, Jean Paul obeyed his dear Madeleine. He

went into his room, undressed himself, hung his
trowsers on a nail and began to brush them with all his
might.

Poor trowsers! you are very old, you have come very
far.   You were not always carefully shut up in a good
trunk, but on foot, always on foot.   Jean Paul did not
think of that.   He brushed and brushed, till he was
bathed in perspiration.   Let us leave him at his work.

Mme. Bienfait and Madeleine talked together while
arranging their apartment.

"Mamma," Madeline said suddenly, "you know that
I must go to the washhouse this morning; I told my
mistress I should not come to work before the afternoon.   You are not strong enough to do the washing.
I must do it this week.   I will call Jean Paul; he must
go with me."

She ran out of the room.   In a minute she returned,
bursting with laughter.   She wanted to speak; she
writhed; the tears ran from her eyes, and she was
obliged to sit down.

"What is the matter, my child? what is it?"

"Oh, mamma!" said Madeleine, still laughing, "I
shall never be able to tell you."   And she laughed until
she cried.

"When you can explain yourself, I shall be able perhaps to understand."   Mme. Bienfait spoke seriously,
took the broom and began to sweep.

"No, I never can; I am laughing too much."   Madeleine tried to control herself.   "Well, mamma, I knocked
at Jean Paul's door.   I called Jean Paul.   'Well, Madeleine,' he answered.   'Come to the washhouse quick!'
'I can't, Madeleine.'   'What! you can't!'   'No.'   'Why?'

'Because'——" She began to laugh again and could not talk any more.

Mme. Bienfait came over and shook her a little. "Why could he not go to the washhouse? Do tell me?"

"It is because, because——" She burst out laughing, impossible to speak.

Then they heard through the partition the lamenting voice of Jean Paul. "Have pity on me, my good Madame Bienfait!"

Mme. Bienfait called back: "I do not hear what you say, my friend. This foolish Madeleine never stops laughing, and deafens me. Come here and explain yourself."

Jean Paul spoke through the partition, evidently crying, "I can't!"

Mme. Bienfait answered, "What! you can't! What do you mean by saying that?"

"No, mamma, he can't come out of his chamber," said Madeleine, "because——" and off she went again.

"You are intolerable with your foolish laugh, my child," said the mother, who was beginning to laugh herself. "What! Jean Paul, are you fastened in?"

Madeleine made a motion of No—still unable to restrain her laughter. "He cannot come out of his room—because——"

Mme. Bienfait said to Jean Paul in a loud voice, "You are fastened in, then?"

Jean Paul answered, also speaking very loud, "No, I am not fastened in. But it is my trowsers!"

"What is that he says?"

But Madeleine was holding her sides laughing. "He has brushed his trowsers so much——"

Now Mme. Bienfait was getting a little angry with Madeleine. She said, "I do not understand it at all. If you would stop laughing a minute, dear child, and speak reasonably——"

Now Madeleine really tried to restrain herself—but still laughing—"Yesterday you said, mamma, that his trowsers—and then——"

Mme. Bienfait ran out of her room and knocked at Jean Paul's door, Madeleine following her. "Let me see, my boy, what is all this? Has anything strange happened?"

"I can't go out—I have no trowsers," said Jean Paul through the door.

"How is that? What have you done with yours?"

Jean Paul answered, in a very small voice, "I have brushed them so much that they are all in pieces."

"Why did you brush them so hard, you awkward little fellow?"

"Madeleine gave me the brush, and said to me, 'Brush, brush them hard, my little Jean Paul! Brush them as hard as you can!' "

"But, mamma," said Madeleine, screaming with laughter, "I assure you I did not tell him to tear his trowsers."

Jean Paul went on, through the door: "Then to please her, I brushed so hard that I was quite in a perspiration."

Mme. Bienfait interrupted him: "Hand me this unfortunate pair of trowsers; I will try to mend them."

"Oh! you are very good!" said Jean Paul, half opening the door. "There they are, Madame Bienfait."

"What is this?" cried Mme. Bienfait, taking the trowsers.

Jean Paul opened the door again. "Here is the other half; when I went to put them on, they tore in two."

"Why!" cried Mme. Bienfait, examining the trowsers, "they are nothing but rags. It is impossible to do anything with them!" She turned to Madeleine, "Well, my poor child, you have made a nice piece of work here; it is your fault that this boy is a prisoner."

Madeleine put her arms around her mother. "Kiss me, dear mother, and confess that the trowsers must have been very old, and that Jean Paul must have brushed very hard to have reduced them to this state." She took in each hand one of the pieces and began to laugh again.

"I laugh in spite of myself. But I am very much annoyed at feeling that this poor child is hindered from going out and is half naked."

Then Madeleine put her arms around her mother and took her into their room. "Dear mamma," she said, "could you not make a pair of trowsers for our friend out of that little brown woollen petticoat that I had last winter, and which is now so narrow and so short for me?"

"With a great many seams in it, perhaps," said Mme. Bienfait reflecting. "Go and look for it in the wardrobe."

"Here, mamma. If you cut them out, I will sit up this evening and sew them; and besides, I will take advantage of Jean Paul's being kept in the house to ask him for his blouse. I will wash it to-day, with our clothes."

"Then you are going to take away his blouse because he has no pantaloons! This unfortunate child
can't pass the day in this manner, half naked. I will
make him put on the petticoat and saque that he wore
the other day when his clothes were drying; he will be
able at least to leave his room." Mme. Bienfait gathered the things together and carried them to Jean Paul.

When Madeleine started for the washhouse with her
bundle on her arm, Jean Paul came out of his room,
dressed in Mme. Bienfait's and Madeleine's clothes.

"Good-bye, Mademoiselle Jean Paul, my little sister,"
said she to him. "Be very good until I come back. I
have told mamma to hide my father's brushes and
trowsers; I did not know that a brush could be so
dangerous."

She ran away laughing. Jean Paul, laughing also,
followed her; but he remembered his costume, of which
he was ashamed, and ran and took refuge with good
Mme. Bienfait.

"Well, my good friend, you look as if you were
caught in a trap," said she to him. "You will be kept
in the house the whole day; but we will take advantage of it, to write to your mother. That will console
you, won't it? Help me to dust and put the room in
order, and then we will be the sooner done."

MADEMOISELLE JEAN PAUL

137

Chapter XVIII

Jean Paul has a secretary

WHEN all was in nice order, Mme. Bienfait took from her bureau an inkstand and a pen. The ink was dried up. They used more needles and thread here than pens and ink. A little drop of clear water nearly repaired the evil. Meanwhile, Mme. Bienfait looked for something that she could not find. At last she felt in her pocket and took out a sou, and said to Jean Paul,

"Go to the grocer's at the corner, my friend, and bring me back two sheets of paper."

Jean Paul had taken the sou, but he stood motionless as if he had been changed into a statue. Go out! he! dressed as he was! with his bare legs, and his girl's dress. Why, it was impossible, entirely impossible!

Mme. Bienfait began again to look in her drawers. Suddenly she turned to Jean Paul.

"What are you thinking about? Run quick! Ah! poor child, I understand. You are right; remain here; you cannot go out as you are. Everybody would laugh at you. Give me the sou, and I will go myself and buy it."

Jean Paul held the sou tight in his hand.

"You must not think of it, my good madame. Go out for the first time in such weather! you who have

139

been so sick! Don't you hear the wind whistling and the rain falling?"

"But it is quite near here, my boy; do not worry about it, I shall soon be back. Give me my sou."

"Well," said Jean Paul, screwing up his courage, "I would rather go out, than let you go. What would Madeleine say when she came home? People will make fun of me—so much the worse for them! but I would rather bear that, than that you should have your bad cold back again."

While speaking, he went out of the room, and ran along the entry.

"The good little child!" said Mme. Bienfait to herself. She moved Madeleine's workbox in dusting it.

"Here is the letter-paper I have been looking for so long!" said she. "It was on my bureau, under Madeleine's box."

She ran into the entry, and called down the staircase.

"Jean Paul! I have found the letter-paper. Come back at once."

The child had gone down to the last step when he heard Mme. Bienfait's voice. He climbed up the six pair of stairs quick as a cat, and came into his friend's room, smiling, but out of breath.

Paper, pen, and ink were ready. Mme. Bienfait seated herself at the table, placed the sheet of paper before her, and dipped her pen in the ink.

"Well, my little friend, I am waiting now. You have only to tell me what I am to write. I must begin with 'My dear mamma,' mustn't I?"

"Oh! you know better than I what to put on that nice white paper!" answered Jean Paul. "My words would spoil it. Write the letter according to your own notion: it will be much better written."

"But, my boy," said Mme. Bienfait, laughing, "I have nothing to say to your mother; I do not know her. Besides, a letter from me would not give her the same pleasure as one from her dear Jean Paul."

"I don't know what to say," sighed Jean Paul. "Not even how to commence it."

"Oh, yes," said Mme. Bienfait. "Imagine that this sheet of paper is a little fairy, who will go with it to Escaladios, find your mother, and repeat to her all that you have told her here. Come, speak!"

"Oh, little sheet of paper," said the child, clasping his hands, "tell my mother that Jean Paul is so happy in sending her some money. Tell her it is not Jean Paul's fault, that he has not sent any before. He had not any except at Bordeaux. But you must know, beloved mother, that I have forgiven the wicked thief, as you taught me to do; therefore I ought not to speak of it even to you."

"Not so fast," said Mme. Bienfait, laughing.

"And then, mamma," continued Jean Paul, "you must know that the good God has sent me a mother, who is as good as you, and whom I love very much, but not as much as you, my first real, darling mother; and then a little sister, named Madeleine, who is so good also! and they take great care of me. I live in the next room to them. Do not be afraid, mamma, Jean Paul is no longer alone——

"Oh, but a letter is not like that, I am sure, good Madame Bienfait!"

"Go on," said the good woman, still writing.

He began again:

"And then, mamma, I am very much worried; who goes to bring water since I left? You are not so pale, I hope, dear mamma. I wish I could kiss your dear face, and hug my sisters also. Do not let little Marie forget me; she must be quite big now.

"Mamma, the mice are very well; they send their compliments to you and my sisters. The cat was very near eating them, only they hid themselves under my bed; then he ate a gray one. I was very much frightened.

"Darling mother, I send you fourteen francs. I say my prayers every day, and every Sunday I take my pretty book to church."

Jean Paul stopped, blushed, and then began again:

"Oh, dear mother, your little Jean Paul believes that if you had seen him all the time since he left you, you would not be displeased with him."

Mme. Bienfait put down the pen, and drew the child towards her.

"That means that you have behaved well since you left her, doesn't it?"

She kissed him affectionately.

"Is it finished?" said she.

"You must put, 'Mamma, pray to the good God, if you please, for my new mamma and sister, for I do not know how to thank them. Mamma, your little Jean Paul asks the good God to bless you, my dear little sisters, the house, the animals, and all the country.'

"That is all, madame," said Jean Paul, wiping his eyes.

"I am going to give her our address, so that your mother may know where to write."

"What a good idea!" said Jean Paul, clapping his hands.

"And then on Sunday I will give the letter and the money to Monsieur Bienfait, who will take charge of it, and put it in the post-office."

About six o'clock at nightfall, Madeleine came back from the washhouse. Jean Paul had been running along the entry for half an hour, going from Mme. Bienfait's room to the head of the staircase, listening, then calling, then listening, then going back again.

At last, he thought he heard steps at the foot of the staircase, and leaning over the balustrade, he called out,

"Madeleine, is it you?"

"Here I am! here I am!" she said.

Jean Paul went down four steps at a time, and joined Madeleine at the middle of the first staircase.

"How you are loaded!" said he to her. "Give me that big wet bundle. You are very tired."

Madeleine wanted to keep her bundle, but Jean Paul had already put it on his back, and had rapidly gone up several steps. She ran to get up to him, but he ran faster.than she did, although his petticoat embarrassed him every moment, and soon after she heard him say to Mme. Bienfait,

"Here is your Madeleine, who has come back. Quick! get the soup ready."

"You must eat, my little Madeleine," said he to her when she reached the room. "Eat, and rest yourself. I will hang out the clothes. Don't be uneasy, it will be well done. I have hung them out more than once for my mother."

While speaking, he went all around the table with his bundle of clothes on his back, as if he were looking for something.

"Where are you going? what are you doing?" said Mme. Bienfait to him.

"I am looking for a place to hang the clothes," answered Jean Paul. "At home we have the road, and the bushes, but here———"

"Ah, indeed, you did not think of hanging the clothes in our room—where we have just space enough for our beds and our table?" said Mme. Bienfait. "Look! here is a line, you will find a big nail at one end of the entry near the staircase, and another at the other end."

"That will do," said Jean Paul. "Begin your dinner. Eat, Madame Bienfait, and you also, Madeleine; I will be with you in a minute."

Jean Paul took a chair to fasten the line, and hung the clothes on it; he got up and down a great many times, until all the clothes swung gracefully from one end of the entry to the other; then he went and seated himself at the table where his two friends were already seated.

At the end of the meal, the courageous little Madeleine gaped while eating her cheese, and she leaned her back against her chair, and let her arms fall by her side; she had not the strength to hold them up.

Suddenly she started:

"Oh, mamma," said she, "Jean Paul's trowsers, have

you cut them out for me? I must make them this evening, you know."

"Yes, my dear, I have cut them out, and done more still," answered Mme. Bienfait. "Take them; they are behind you, on the back of your chair."

Madeleine turned around, seized hold of them and examined them all over—Oh joy! the trowsers were cut, basted, sewed and finished.

"Dear mother!" cried Madeleine.

"I knew very well that you would be too tired to make them this evening, my dear," said Mme. Bienfait. "I felt much better to-day, and I have been able to work. We will make the shirt together to-morrow evening."

They bid each other good night, kissed each other, and separated; Jean Paul carrying off his precious trowsers, that he hardly dared to touch, and which he carried carefully folded. He looked at them with respect.

CHAPTER XIX

Jean Paul dines out

AT last the famous Sunday came. It was five
o'clock. The table was set in Mme. Bienfait's
little room. The tablecloth was as white as snow.
Madeleine had set the table. She would not let her
mother help her. She would have let Jean Paul, if he
had been there. "But where is he? What is he doing?
Why does he not come, the naughty boy?"

Jean Paul was in his room, standing, trembling there.
He did not dare to sit down, for fear the blades of
straw might stick in his trowsers. He had on his
white shirt, his new trowsers, and his blouse nicely
washed. He looked at his hands; he had already been
twice to the pump.

"I hope the water in our yard washes well!" thought
he.

For the first time he noticed that there was no look-
ing-glass in his room; he wanted to look at his face
and hair. His heart was beating at the idea of seeing
Madeleine's father. He put his hand on the latch of
the door to open it; but no, he was too much afraid.

If he could have seen through the wall this terrible
father, sitting on an old armchair, looking at his dear
little Madeleine with a smile while she was getting
everything ready for dinner, he would have been less
frightened.

M. Bienfait was still weak; his sufferings had made
146

him pale. He leaned towards the fireplace, and drew the coals together.

"Jean Paul," said Madeleine, "give a stick of wood to father. Oh! how foolish I am," said she, interrupting herself; "I called Jean Paul, as if he were here. But I am really going to call him. I am sure he has come in."

She ran out of the room, and they heard her knocking at her friend's door, and very soon she came back with him, drawing him in with her hand. He was blushing to his ears, and his eyes were fastened on the ground.

Madeleine led him to her father's armchair, and put Jean Paul's hand in her father's.

"Father," said she, "here is our little friend, Jean Paul, who took such good care of mamma."

"Oh, he is a good boy," said Mme. Bienfait.

M. Bienfait pressed Jean Paul's cold and trembling hand very warmly, and held it in his own, as if to warm it. He drew the child still nearer to him.

"Jean Paul," said he to him, "you have been of great service to us; you have behaved to us as if you were our own son, so we love you. But how you tremble! Why, my child, is it because you are afraid of me? Come, raise your head, and look me in the face."

Jean Paul raised his head slowly, and looked at M. Bienfait; then his face brightened with smiles.

"Oh no,"·cried he, "I am not afraid of you; you are just like Madeleine."

And he jumped on M. Bienfait's knees, put his arms around his neck, and kissed him very warmly.

He is right," cried Mme. Bienfait. "Madeleine and you have the same brown eyes, the same mouth, the same hair; indeed you resemble each other very much."

"Ah! well, if I am so much like Madeleine, it may be said that I am not handsome, not handsome at all," looking roguishly at his daughter.

But she, who for a long time had been accustomed to this joke, laughing, threw her arms around her father.

"Naughty, naughty father!" and she smothered him with kisses. Jean Paul remained also on his knees, and continued to caress him. Poor M. Bienfait could scarcely breathe. "You will send me back to the hospital, dear children," said he, smiling with happiness. "Go, you had better set the table."

Jean Paul and Madeleine sprang to the floor, then ran to Mme. Bienfait to give her her share of the kisses, they said. Every plate was wiped ten times, every glass also, and they admired first this, then that. At last they sat down to the table, as M. and Mme. Bienfait said they were dying with hunger.

Never was there a gayer meal. They ate, they drank, they laughed, and they talked of everything: of Jean Paul's mother, of M. and Mme. Fumeron, of my lady and Rosette, and of their new dresses. M. Bienfait talked to Jean Paul of his journey, asked him many questions as to the employment of his time, of his little savings, and so forth. Then he looked at him steadily, and said thoughtfully: "This child will gain his livelihood, you will see."

"How do you know that, darling father?" said

Madeleine, enchanted with the prophecy. "Are you a magician? Can you read faces?"

"Yes," answered M. Bienfait. "I can read fortunes in the face, and in the clothes. Look, little Madeleine, do not this nice white skin, this glossy hair so nicely combed, and these clean clothes, speak to us of order, of care, and even of courage?"

Jean Paul blushed deeply, and looked at Madeleine, who blushed also. Mme. Bienfait changed the conversation.

They finished by drinking a glass of blackberry cordial to the health of the absent. Jean Paul's mother and her four daughters were mentioned so often, that Jean Paul began to believe he was again in Escaladios; but he had never before seen such a feast.

Chapter XX

Jean Paul's first step in literature

THE week finished well. The weather was fine. M. Bienfait was able to go back to his workroom, at first for a few hours each day, and then for the whole day. Jean Paul went out diligently with his little mice, and his receipts were so good, that on Saturday evening he was able to give to Mme. Bienfait three francs that he had saved for his mother.

"Dear father, will you let Jean Paul come on Sunday

when you are giving me lessons?" said Madeleine, just as Jean Paul left after bidding them good night.

"But——" said M. Bienfait.

"Oh, but I beg you to do so," returned Madeleine.

"I would willingly," said M. Bienfait, "if that would please you; however——"

Madeleine did not listen any longer, she ran after Jean Paul.

"You will come to-morrow at eleven o'clock exactly, won't you, my little Jean Paul?"

"What for?" said Jean Paul.

"You will see! remember, eleven o'clock exactly," repeated Madeleine.

"Yes, yes," said our friend.

Jean Paul was returning from church, when he heard the clock strike eleven. He remembered the promise he had made to Madeleine the evening before, and hurried on. On going into Mme. Bienfait's room, he was quite astonished to see Madeleine seated at the table leaning over a book, which she was reading aloud. Her father, who was seated alongside of her, was listening to her, and correcting her occasionally. She nodded to Jean Paul, but without stopping. M. Bienfait pointed to a chair near Madeleine. Jean Paul seated himself there without daring to say a word, or move. He remained so quiet that by degrees, he heard nothing but hou, hou—ou, ou, and then he did not hear anything at all. He nodded to M. Bienfait and Madeleine, but luckily they did not perceive it.

All at once he awoke suddenly. Madeleine had stopped reading.

"It is your turn now, Jean Paul," said she. "Father,

are you not going to have the goodness to teach him to read? I will write while you teach him, and I will apply myself so closely, that my writing will be as well done as if you were looking over the page. You must know, Jean Paul," added she, "before my father's sickness, he gave me a long lesson every Sunday, and mamma made me study every evening."

Jean Paul sat motionless, with open mouth; he rubbed his eyes to try to understand what was going on.

M. Bienfait turned over the leaves of a book.

"Do you know how to read, my boy?"

•"Not much," said Jean Paul.

"Oh, father!" said Madeleine, raising her head, which was bent over her copybook, and interrupting a magnificent line of Y's. "Make him read the first story of the .book, that one about Little Roger. It is so pretty, and so easy."

"Willingly," said M. Bienfait. He put the book on the table, and pointed with his finger to the first words.

Jean Paul began: "Our—Our—"

"No, my child, a, a."

Jean Paul stammered, "A, a father—"

"Oh! no, a lit—"

Said Jean Paul, "A father—"

"A father!" cried M. Bienfait. "Why, where do you see father?" He read: "A l-i-t-t-l-e—little."

Jean Paul continued: "A father, our, no, little." He began again: "A father—Who—"

Madeleine interrupted him, stopped, then striking with her hand upon the table. "It is not that, Jean Paul! A little boy."

Jean Paul began again, pointing with his finger, and saying slowly: "A—little—boy—who—who art in heaven."

M. Bienfait corrected him: "A little boy, named Roger; n-a-m-e-d, named. Tell me where you see, who art in heaven?"

"But do you not see," said Jean Paul, with tears in his eyes, "that I only know how to read Our Father in my book. I will go and get it for you. I have just put it in my room."

M. Bienfait burst out laughing. "Well, then, my poor boy, you do not know how to read at all?"

"Not much!" said Jean Paul, sadly. "I told you so."

"Poor little Jean Paul!" said Madeleine, smiling sweetly at him. "The little you know is better than nothing. Come, you will learn very quickly; it is not so difficult as you think."

"In the meantime, my dear Madeleine," said her father, "It will be impossible to teach him at the same time as you. Let us see. Where is your A B C book? I will put him at ba, be, bi, bo, bu. That will be enough for to-day."

The A B C book was found and the syllables repeated very often by M. Bienfait. Jean Paul began to study, or at least he put his book on the table before him, and was quiet. The silence was so great, that nothing was heard but the movement of Madeleine's pen.

Jean Paul got up suddenly: "Madeleine, I believe it is quite clear to-day. I must go out with my lady."

"Why," cried Madeleine, "It is pouring—don't you

hear the rain falling on the roof? What are you thinking of? Do you know your lesson?"

"Oh no! but I have not time to learn it."

"What! not time?"

"That is to say—my mice—I think they must be hungry, I am going to feed them." He half opened the door.

"Jean Paul," said Madeleine, seriously, "I shall be quite angry with you, if you do not come back immediately."

"I will be back again," Jean Paul said, going out. "That is, that is—well, yes."

"I think that the mice do not want feeding," said M. Bienfait, "as much as Jean Paul wants to move his legs. My dear Madeleine, your friend will not profit much by our Sunday lesson. Poor child! accustomed as he is to run through the streets from morning till night! How can you expect him to apply himself to study?"

"Oh, darling father, I hope that he'll—But here he is. Come, Jean Paul, take your book again quickly. We have but a quarter of an hour more; at twelve o'clock the lesson will be finished."

There was silence again. Jean Paul gaped once, twice, three, and four times. "Madeleine, where is your mamma?" said he.

Madeleine answered in a low voice: "Hush! study! At church. Hush!"

Jean Paul gaped again. There was a moment of silence. Then he said in a loud voice, "It is Sunday! it is time to put on the soup. Had I not better go and get the coal at the shop?   When your mamma comes in she will find——"

Madeleine replied, "We have enough!   Learn your lesson!   Hush!"

M. Bienfait had taken up a book.   He pretended to be reading, but he was looking at the children, and could not restrain a smile.

Jean Paul fixed his eyes a moment on his book, then he said to Madeleine: "How wet your mamma will be!"

"Hush! hush!"

"Are you sure that she has an umbrella?"

"Yes, she has an umbrella, and a big one too—But do study now, Jean Paul!"

The clock struck, and Jean Paul jumped quickly from his chair: "Twelve o'clock! twelve o'clock! the lesson is over!"   He stretched his arms over his head. "How hard we have worked!   I could not have stood it any longer.   I was more tired than if I had walked a dozen leagues."

M. Bienfait put his book down.   "Poor child! and you do not know your lesson!   If you had learnt it, you would not have been so tired, I am sure."

"Oh, do not scold him, darling father," said Madeleine.   "I am going to do the same for him, as mother did for me.   Every evening I will give him a short lesson, and on Sundays you can see what progress he has made."

"But, Madeleine," said Jean Paul, "Don't you know you are always so tired in the evening, it would be bad for you?"

Madeleine pointed her finger at him, laughing.   "Oh the naughty, lazy boy!   You see, father, he does not want to learn to read. But so much the worse, Monsieur Jean Paul," added she, firmly, although laughing still. "I want you to learn to read. Do you hear? Now, go get the mice and show them to father; it is raining so hard, we must amuse ourselves a little at home."

Mme. Bienfait came back, not very wet. She wanted Jean Paul to stay and lunch with them. Madeleine clapped her hands with ·delight. There was no more talking of books, nor reading, nor lessons. Jean Paul amused them, and they passed the day gaily,

Chapter XXI

A good lesson

THE next evening at eight o'clock, Madeleine held her work in her hand; while leaning over Jean Paul, she showed him with her right hand, pointing with her needle, the letters he must say. Jean Paul looked red, his hair looked like brushwood, and his eyes were quite swollen; he had been crying.

Madeleine was saying, "Well, go on, Jean Paul. B-a, ba; b-i, bi; b-o, bo. Go on! are you asleep?"

"Well," grumbled Jean Paul, "these books I have always found make people either go to sleep or cry."

"But I thought that you used to take excellent lessons with your mother. Did the little book at Escaladios make you sleep and cry?"

"Not always—but very often." He gaped.

Madeleine was a little dissatisfied. "Come, go to bed, my poor Jean Paul! but you must come here to-morrow, at half past seven o'clock. Do you promise to do so? and will you try to learn a good lesson?"

Jean Paul kissed her. "You are not angry with me, dear teacher, are you?"

The next evening, when our friend came to see Madeleine, he had already put on his school expression; that is to say, he looked downcast, and half asleep. There was no sleeping at Mme. Bienfait's. M. Bienfait was busy mending a delicate key of a beautiful workbox; he was trying it in the lock. Mme. Bienfait was mending a greatcoat, and Madeleine had a bundle of linen by her that she was mending.

As Jean Paul softly opened the door of the room, he heard the sound of voices speaking with animation. One would have said that M. and Mme. Bienfait and Madeleine spoke all at once, and that the subject was very interesting. But as soon as they saw our friend they were silent, and Jean Paul thought he saw Madeleine hide something quickly under her bundle of work.

Jean Paul did not say good evening to his friends, he had not strength enough to do so, but he offered his good fat face to each one to kiss.

"Ah!" said Madeleine to him, "we are going to have a good lesson to-day, I am sure."

Jean Paul seated himself beside her, took the A B C book from the table, opened it slowly and commenced with a distressed voice: b—then he heaved a great sigh; a—another sigh, ba. He sighed again and stopped, then said b again; he sighed a, he sighed ba. Still sighing, "A—oh, no, that one has a little dot above it; b-i—bi——"

Madeleine leaned towards him, and passed her finger along the line. "No, you always say, b-a—ba! it is b-e—be, b——"

Jean Paul began to cry: "But how can you expect me to know them? They are all alike, excepting this one with a dot, and that's so small."

Madeleine left her work. "All alike, Jean Paul! a-e-i-o-u are all alike?"

Jean Paul was still half crying. "There is so little difference, it is not worth speaking of: I have not good eyes." He jumped up quickly. "Oh, Madeleine, how you have muddied your boots to-day! and your mamma also went out to-day, and I see one, two, three, four, five, six shoes that are drying in the chimney corner. I am going to clean them in the entry, so as not to make any dust. Will you leave the door open?"

Madeleine looked quite dissatisfied. She was going to scold him, but no, she smiled.

"Jean Paul," said she to him, "let the shoes alone, and only think of your lesson. Listen," added she quickly. "If you read well this evening, I promise you a reward." She made a motion with her head to her father and mother. "And a nice reward! Won't it be so, father?"

Jean Paul, still standing up, said, "But, my poor Madeleine, what good is there in learning and knowing these ugly little black things? We can pray very well to the good God, love our friends, and serve them, without that! And then you can go to heaven without knowing them; isn't it so?"

Now Mr. Bienfait interrupted his work and looked at Jean Paul. "It is certain that knowing how to read will not be of much service to us in Paradise, but it may help us to get there. And I assure you that knowing how to read is very useful in this world, every day of our lives."

Madeleine said quickly, "And I will give you proof of it in an instant, Jean Paul; yes, I will prove it to you at once."

Jean Paul reseated himself, and began to sigh again.

Madeleine said, "Ah! I have thought of a good plan! Go and get your prayer book, Jean Paul. I am going to teach you to read in another way. It will be very funny."

Jean Paul went out, and came back again with his book. While he was absent getting it, his three friends began to talk together gaily. They were silent when he came in—What could be the matter?

Madeleine said, "Look in your book for the Lord's Prayer at the place you are in the habit of reading."

"Here it is," said Jean Paul turning over the leaves of the book.

"Well, look at the first word, 'Our.' How do you say it?"

"Our."

Madeleine took a book from the table. "Here is the history of Little Roger. If you show me all the 'Ours' that are in this story, without missing one of them, you shall have a reward."

"What reward?—tell me!"

"No!"

"Please tell me!" He went around the table and begged M. and Mme. Bienfait to tell him what was the reward Madeleine intended to give him; but both of them put their fingers on their lips, and did not answer.

"You will never get it," said Madeleine, "if you run about, instead of studying."

So Jean Paul sat down again, and took his book. "Oh, very well! This will be a great deal more amusing than ba, bo, bi, bu. Madeleine, here is one of those things."

"Of those what?" She looked. "Why no; that is not our—that is out; pay attention!"

Jean Paul put the books on the table alongside of him. One of the fingers of his right hand he placed on the famous "Our" which was to serve him as a model, one of the fingers of his other hand was searching line by line through the story of Little Roger. He was looking so attentively that his eyes seemed nearly starting from his head. He jumped up from his chair: "Ah! now this time I have found one of them, and a good one!"

"Yes, a real our. Go on."

Jean Paul pointed with his finger: "Two, three; aren't they, Madeleine?"

"Yes, yes, the reward is near."

Jean Paul went on: "Four, five, six—No, this is not one of them. Five, six seven, eight. Oh, Madeleine, I have done. I have got to the end of the history of Little Roger. My reward! my reward!"

But Madeleine looked through the book attentively: "You have missed two of them; you must look again, and show them to me once more."

"Oh dear!" he sighed. "Let me see, I will begin again; one, two, three 'ours,' four, five, six, seven——"

"No, you must show the word and say, 'our,' every time you meet it."

Now Jean Paul was quite animated: "Our, our, our, our; no, not that one; our, our, our, our, our, that's all!"

Madeleine counted on her fingers: "You have only said nine of them, there are ten. Jean Paul, my friend, begin again."

"Ugh! I can stand it no longer——"

M. Bienfait interrupted: "Madeleine, I beg you will excuse his saying the tenth one. Look, the poor fellow is all in a perspiration. He has done very well this evening, and now I think you can speak to him of his reward."

Madeleine hesitated. "Well, I will excuse you this evening, Jean Paul, but I want to tell you that to-morrow, you must find all the 'fathers,' and not miss one of them."

Jean Paul was wriggling in his chair. "Yes, yes, yes! The reward!"

"And you must look again for all the 'ours' of to-day."

"All the 'ours,' yes. The reward!"

But Madeleine kept on, very seriously: "And day after to-morrow you must look for all the 'whos,' and all the 'ours.' "

Jean Paul cried out very loud, quite beside himself: "All the 'fathers,' all the 'ours,' yes, yes!"

"Oh," said Mme. Bienfait, "You keep him too long in suspense; let us see the reward."

Madeleine lifted up her work, and took from under it a small newspaper.

Jean Paul turned away. "Is that the reward? a paper with those little black things on it to read! Thank you, I do not want it. If I had known it, I would not have found a single 'our.' "

"Wait, wait," said Madeleine slyly. "It is a story I am going to read to you."

"Are there fairies in it?"

"Better than that. Father, read it, I beg of you. You read better than I do." She passed the paper to M. Bienfait. Unfolding it, he began to read. "A very useful tale, is the name of the story."

Jean Paul leaned back in his chair as if he intended to go to sleep.

M. Bienfait began again:

"We hear from Bordeaux that yesterday there was a great crowd collected in the street. A lady very elegantly dressed, was standing before a jeweller's window, admiring the chains and bracelets. A young boy in a working dress came near her, and seemed to admire them also. Suddenly, she turned around quickly, and cried out; it seemed to her that some one was feeling in her pocket. The thief ran away, or rather wanted to run away; but his legs became entangled in the long purple silk train of this elegant lady, and he fell full length on the pavement. Before he could get up, the passers-by flocked around him, and a police officer put his hand upon him. The most singular part of the affair was that it had only been a few hours since the young man had come out of the jail of our town, where he had passed six months; and the same police officer who had arrested him the first time, arrested him now. They searched him immediately, and they found in his pocket a watch, a bracelet, a lace barbe, which the elegant lady recognized as hers, and a little bag of coarse linen tied with a red string, and which contained a great many small pieces of silver money."

Jean Paul came near the table and interrupted:

"How was this bag made? Did they say that Jane was written in red letters on the prettiest side? It was my sister Alice who embroidered it for mamma, when she learnt how to mark. Oh, tell me, tell me, my good M. Bienfait."

Madeleine took the newspaper from her father, and said very calmly: "Little father, you are tired; that is enough for to-day; you can finish the story to-morrow."

Jean Paul seized the newspaper. "Oh, my little Madeleine! I beseech you to read me what comes after." But Madeleine put her hand on her throat. "I am quite hoarse also; you made me talk so much during the lesson—I cannot speak another word." She hid her desire to laugh.

Jean Paul took the newspaper to Mme. Bienfait, and knelt before her. "Oh dear Madame Bienfait, I beg you to read the end of this story."

The stern Madeleine said quickly, "You know very well that mamma's lungs have been weak since she had the bronchitis last winter, and that she still coughs, and cannot read aloud." She took the newspaper and folded it in such a way, that the letter from Bordeaux was underneath, and handed it to Jean Paul. "Since no one can read it for you, read it yourself, my little friend. Here is the place where my father left off: pieces of silver money."

"Oh! how cruel you are!" cried Jean Paul. "You know very well that I can't make out a single word."

Madeleine rose and stood opposite to him, with her arms crossed.

"Ah, well, Monsieur Jean Paul, is it not useful to know how to read?"

"Yes, yes."

"Will you tell me again, that you will not learn?"

"No, no, never."

"Will you study well?"

"Yes, yes, perfectly."

Then Madeleine seated herself again. "Well, you are a good boy, and—you can go to bed."

Jean Paul ready to cry, stamped on the floor. "Cruel, cruel Madeleine! The end of the story!"

"What story?" said Madeleine. But M. Bienfait made a motion to her to begin to read again; Madeleine, smiling, unfolded the paper, and continued: "A bag of coarse linen, tied with a red string, and containing many little pieces of silver money. When the police officer saw the bag, and its contents, he stood still for a moment, as if he wished to recall something to his memory. It appeared that when the robber had been arrested for the first time, some one had laid claim to a little bag containing money, and that the policeman had searched from the top to the bottom of the miserable lodging house of the thief, without being able to discover anything. 'Who then claimed this little bag?' said the policeman. He thought that he remembered that it was a poor child, that he had met on the bridge of Cubesac—but where can he be found now?"

Jean Paul interrupted: "It was I, here I am!"

Madeleine motioned to him to be quiet, and went on:

"It was a question where the thief had put the money, and how he could find it so easily, so soon after coming out of prison. It was thought that he must have an accomplice who had helped him in his robberies.

"Our rascal, escorted by twenty curious persons, was taken back to his prison, which he never ought to have quitted."

"Is that all?" asked M. Bienfait.

"No, there are still a few lines: It is said the same evening, thanks to the active search of the police, the accomplice of our young thief was arrested. There were found in his house jewels, porte-monnaies, handkerchiefs, umbrellas, and a quantity of other things that will be returned to the owners."

Jean Paul jumped up quickly: "Thank you, my little Madeleine; good-bye, good mamma Bienfait; good-bye, my good friend; good-bye, Madelichon."

"What! good-bye! but where are you going?" they cried out, all together.

"I am going to bed,—but to-morrow before day-light, I am going to Bordeaux."

"To Bordeaux!"

"I am going to claim my little bag. Don't be uneasy, I will return."

"What, you are going a hundred and twenty leagues, and the same back, and all for fifteen francs!" Said M. Bienfait.

"Oh, I know the way very well." Jean Paul was counting on his fingers. "In five or six weeks, you will see your little Jean Pual returning with his bag."

"But you can have the money in a week, and remain quietly here."

"Is that possible!" Jean Paul was astonished.

"You will only have to write a letter to the judge at Bordeaux, in which you can explain to him how your bag is made, and you can give him your address. You see that the police officer remembers you and your claim."

Now Jean Paul was embarrassed: "Oh, but I don't know how to write."

Madeleine said quickly, "I will write for him, father. You see" (she turned towards Jean Paul) "it is a good thing to know how to write."

Jean Paul clasped his hands:

"Oh! if you will write for me, I will promise to learn all that you want."

"No, I had better write, my child." M. Bienfait thought a moment. "First of all, Jean Paul must tell me exactly how this famous bag is made, that will prove that it belongs to him. Madeleine, give me a piece of paper and pencil, I will copy it to-morrow in my letter. Now, Jean Paul, tell me how your bag was made."

Jean Paul opened his eyes very wide, and spoke very quickly: "It is quite a small linen bag; there are letters on the outside, because one day as it was my mother's fête, then Alice did not know how to mark, she went every day to the neighbors who taught her, and then for my mother's fête, and to put her thimble and thread in the bag, and Jane which was my mother's name was written on it, and then when I left the country, mother gave it to me to put my money in, and that's all."

M. Bienfait sat with his pencil in the air: "If it were possible to understand a word of all this rigmarole, I would give twenty francs." Madeleine burst out laughing.

"Come," said M. Bienfait, "This famous bag is——?"

"Is mine; my mother gave it to me."

"That was not what I asked you; is it gray or white?"

"It is yellow," said Jean Paul, "And made of the stuff shirts are made of."

Now M. Bienfait was writing. "Of linen, then? Is it big?"

"About as big as my two hands, and on the outside is marked 'Jane' with red cotton in big letters."

"And the inside?"

"And the inside is yellow also, with letters which do not seem very well done; that is the under part."

"I did not ask you that, I know very well what is on the wrong side. What was in it? How many pieces, and what kind of pieces? The thief may perhaps have taken some of them, but the judge will understand that very well."

Jean Paul counted on his fingers: "There were six twenty-sous pieces, and eighteen little ten-sous pieces; no ugly sous."

"Well, my child, that will do, I will send this description to——" He stopped and reflected, then he spoke to his wife. "Tell me what address shall I put, my dear; I cannot put 'The Judge, at Bordeaux,' the letter would not perhaps arrive there."

Mme. Bienfait thought a moment. "When you take back M. Aubersart's box, you can perhaps ask his advice. I believe he is a judge also, and he is such a good man."

"Oh yes, whenever I do any work for him, he always says 'Good day, Monsieur Bienfait! How do you do, Monsieur Bienfait?' That is a golden thought of yours, my wife. But my lock is not yet ready; it is a fine piece of work, and I must not spoil the wood. Go, children, run away, let me do my work. This box must be mended this evening, so that to-morrow at nine o'clock, I may be at Monsieur Aubersart's."

M. Bienfait raised the wick of the lamp and began his work.

Madeleine said good night to her parents, and went into her narrow room.

Jean Paul said good night also, and went towards the door; but he rested his hand on the handle of the lock. After a few minutes, Mme. Bienfait, astonished at not having heard the noise of the shutting of the door, turned around, and saw Jean Paul.

"Well, why don't you go to bed?" said she to him.

"That poor unfortunate fellow, still in prison, that makes me unhappy." He sighed.

M. Bienfait said gently, "What do you mean, my child? Crime must be punished."

"But," said Jean Paul, "He has not repented, since he began again immediately; the good God will not forgive him!"

"Go to bed, my dear little boy," said Mme. Bienfait. "Don't distress yourself."

Jean Paul hesitated. "It would perhaps be better not to write for this little bag, and to tell this poor creature we would give it to him, provided he repented," he went on in a low voice. "I would give my little bag to the good God, in order that he might give him repentance."

"You are a good boy, Jean Paul," said M. Bienfait, "Come and kiss me. This money belongs more to your mother than to you, my dear child; let us try to get it again. You are going to pray to God to-night—pray for this criminal. You are right, he is greatly to be pitied."

Just then Madeleine returned to the room. "And to think no one has thanked me! It was however I, Jean Paul, who brought this wonderful newspaper from the workroom. It was the head woman who ran to buy it, when madame was out. I did not listen at first, but when I heard Bordeaux! then I thought of Jean Paul, and listened a little. I did right, didn't I?"

"Indeed you did!" cried Jean Paul.

Mme. Bienfait took up her scissors. "We will cut

out the story of the little bag from the newspaper and keep it."

"Oh! give it to me," begged Jean Paul, "that I may put it in my prayer book. It shall be the first thing that I will read. Oh! and then let me give the remainder to my mice to eat. Dear little newspaper, that has given us so much pleasure! You would like, would you not, to go into the white stomachs of my lady and Rosette?"

But M. and Mme. Bienfait were speaking together: "Children, children, good night, and go to bed; it is half-past ten o'clock."

The two children kissed each other, and went into their rooms.

Chapter XXII

A case of conscience

MME. BIENFAIT drew near the fire, and moved the cinders. It was the month of March, but it was still very cold. The nights were freezing. M. Bienfait also drew his chair near the fireplace, and the two began their work again. Mme. Bienfait was mending the old greatcoat of her husband, putting patches on the lining, first sewing one sleeve and then the other. The more she did, the more she seemed to find to do. M. Bienfait was putting on and taking off his little lock, screwing and filing; the little key would not fit.

To amuse themselves while working, these honest people chatted. They spoke of their child, of their children—for Jean Paul had really won their hearts.

"He was very pale this evening," said Mme. Bienfait.

"Do you think so?" said M. Bienfait, "He has a good complexion, however."

"He has become very pale and thin since we have known him. I often think he does not eat every day."

"Can it be possible?"

"I have often wanted him to eat a little meat with us; at first he accepted, now he always refuses; he is afraid to deprive us of it, I am sure."

"He could not live without eating, however; do you know about how much he makes a day?" M. Bienfait was troubled.

His wife hesitated. "I have often thought—and I wanted to ask you—if it would not be disagreeable to you, if I were to ask him to give me every day what he spends in those bad, detestable eating houses, and then I would give him his dinner."

"If I were well off, I would like much better to give him his dinner for nothing."

"We must think of it seriously, before he gets into the habit of eating here; for after all, poor child, the days that he would not make anything, we would have him to eat with us, just the same; always when he receives a good deal of money, he puts it aside for his mother. I would not touch his little hoard—and now, Madeleine wants new chemises, and she must have a summer dress, also."

"Ah!" said M. Bienfait sighing, "our illness this winter has not made us rich!"

Let them talk, these good parents, and let us go into Madeleine's little room. It is very easy, for the door is open all night. The little room is so narrow that Madeleine would suffocate if it were shut.

Madeleine has been in bed for a long time, but it was in vain that she shut her eyes, and breathed hard, to persuade herself that she slept. She had been so agitated all the evening, that her heart still beat, and she heard in her head, "toc, toc, toc." It is very tiresome not to be able to sleep. But all at once she forgot her trouble, she heard her name and Jean Paul's pronounced by her father in the next room. She listened.

"Oh, it is too true," said she to herself, "that Jean Paul is badly fed!"

And then she remembered having seen him pick up a crust of bread from off a heap of dirt. "Oh! mother," said she to herself, "what a good idea to have him to dine with us! Oh! papa would like it, wouldn't he?" she still spoke to herself. "But I do not want new chemises, I will mend my old ones. Oh! what will they decide upon?" Her heart beat harder than ever, she listened and listened.

But then a small voice within began to talk quite low. At first, Madeleine hardly heard it.

"Madeleine," this still small voice said, "is it right to listen to what your father and mother are saying, when they think that you are asleep?"

But Madeleine answered herself, "It is not my fault that I cannot sleep. I have done all that I am able to do to make myself sleep."

"That's true," answered the small voice, "but still you are not sleeping, your good parents think that you are asleep, and they are talking as if they were alone, and you are wide awake listening to them."

"Mother! my little mother! I am not asleep!" called out Madeleine in her sweet voice.

"You are not sick, my dear?" answered good Mme. Bienfait, tenderly.

"No, dear mamma," said Madeleine, who just then came into the room with her petticoat and little shawl.

She threw her arms around her father's neck.

"Forgive me, father and mother, I have heard all that you said. I could not sleep, and I listened to you without thinking that it was deceiving you a little, but all at once my good angel whispered it to me in a low voice."

Mme. Bienfait drew her towards her and kissed her:

"My dearest child, this voice that you heard within was better than an angel; it was the good God Him‹ self Who spoke to you."

"Oh! my dear parents, since I have heard you, I ask you with all my heart to give a dinner every day to our dear Jean Paul. I know that he spends barely from five to six sous every day for his food. Let him bring this to you, and give him every morning a good cup of coffee and milk, and a good dinner the same as ours, every evening. Ah! little mamma, I know that will cost you more than six sous a day, but you are so good! and then, mamma, I do not want either chemises or dresses. The old ones will do yet, and I will mend them well, and that is so much gained. Ah! dear papa and mamma, let us all be quiet, and let us listen to that voice which speaks from the bottom of the heart: 'Have pity on him who has no father, and who is far away from his mother.'" She looked at them. "Mamma's eyes say yes, and papa's too." She clapped her hands. "How good you both are! I am going at once to wake Jean Paul. I can't wait until to-morrow to tell him the good news."

Mme. Bienfait caught her hand. "Foolish child! it is half-past eleven o'clock! Let him sleep, and you go to bed and sleep too, and that immediately."

Madeleine gave the most affectionate kisses to her dear parents, jumped into her bed, covered herself up well, and now slept soundly.

CHAPTER XXIII

Jean Paul has a plate set for him

AT seven o'clock the next morning, Madeleine knocked at the partition separating their room from Jean Paul's.

"Get up, get up," said she, "breakfast is in this way."

"What?" Jean Paul answered through the partition. "Who is waiting for me? What?"

"Come quick! everybody is ready. It is a bad habit to come late to meals."

Jean Paul came in half asleep, and rubbing his eyes. "What have I done, my little Madeleine? What is the matter?"

"What is the matter? Why, you are making us all wait; the milk and coffee both will be cold. Look! the toast is burning."

"Ah! but how is it my fault?" said Jean Paul with open eyes and mouth.

Madeleine was scraping the toast with a knife, and putting her head in the fireplace, that Jean Paul might not see that she was laughing. "Why, you know very well, Jean Paul, that it was agreed last night, that you were to breakfast and dine with us every day. What! don't you remember?"

Madeleine poured out the coffee and milk into the cups. "Yes, Monsieur Jean Paul, it was agreed that you should give mamma six sous every day to pay for

176

your food. What, is it true that you do not remember it?" She laughed.

Jean Paul replied very seriously: "I suppose it was during the reading lessons. I slept a little then."

"Well, well, I see that you begin to remember."

Jean Paul thought a while, then said very quickly, "Ah! but no! yesterday I did not sleep. It was all the 'ours,' and then the reward, and then the newspaper, and then the little bag!"

During this time Madeleine had finished preparing her father's and mother's breakfast. Then she poured out a full bowl of milk, added the coffee and sugar to it, put a chair to the table, and said, making a graceful curtsy to Jean Paul: "Your breakfast is ready."

But Jean seemed neither to see nor hear.

"This is for you, my little Jean Paul," Madeleine said to him in her most caressing voice. "Eat it at once; the coffee will clear your head, and bring back your memory."

Jean Paul still stood at the door. "Oh, it is not possible—you know very well, Madeleine, I can't eat here."

Madeleine had helped herself, and was beginning to eat. "You do not like coffee and milk?"

"I liked it at Escaladios on Christmas day and at Easter. But really it is too good for me. A piece of bread is a good enough meal for Jean Paul."

"Too good for you! Look, we all take it." She pointed to her father and mother.

"Oh! that's another thing! you, you are Monsieur Bienfait; you, you are Madeleine's mother; you, you are Madeleine; while, as for me, I am only Jean Paul."

"Come, dear boy," said Mme. Bienfait, "take your coffee while it is warm; it will be a pleasure to us to see you make a good breakfast."

"Sit down, Jean Paul," said M. Bienfait. "Come, my friend."

Jean Paul seated himself at the table and began to eat. Then he stopped suddenly: "But all this will cost you a great deal of money every day," said he. "Oh, Monsieur Bienfait, really I can't eat this way every day! Madeleine, is it true that I promised to come every day to breakfast and dinner? I must have been without heart to have said so; once I thought you were very rich, but since your mother was sick"—— He interrupted himself, and turned very red— "I will not say you are poor, but in short"—— he blushed more and more.

Madeleine was blushing also. "You can truly say it, little Jean Paul, that we had no money left in the house, and that we did not know what to do, and that you helped us very much."

Jean Paul interrupted her: "It is all the same, Madeleine, I can't come every day, and eat you out of house and home in this way. It would cost you enormously—and I was to give you only six sous for the trouble! I could not have promised that, my Madeleine."

"I did not say that you had promised; I said that it was agreed. Well, yes, papa, mamma, and I (for they consulted Madeleine), we agreed that Jean Paul should breakfast and dine here."

"But where was I then?"

"In your bed sleeping soundly." Madeleine came

up to him affectionately. "But now my dear little Jean Paul must promise us never to miss coming morning or evening. Do not say no, dear friend. You would then prevent us from receiving that great blessing that the good God has promised to those who feed the hungry—and you are always hungry, always hungry, aren't you?"

Jean Paul blushed and answered, looking affectionately at all his friends, "Not now, at any rate."

"Well, now it is decided." Madeleine gaily offered her open hand to Jean Paul. "Take my hand, Jean Paul." He obeyed. "And now go take my father's and mother's hands, and remember that this is a solemn promise. Every day at seven o'clock in the morning, and at eight o'clock in the evening you must come here. Good-bye! Why, I had almost forgotten your luncheon! Look! here is a nice piece of bread."

"Well, that is too much. Don't be uneasy, Madeleine, I can exhibit my mice to the bakers and confectioners, and get a piece of stale cake from them." Jean Paul put back the piece of bread in the cupboard. "I would like to go out with my lady to make some more money. But it is not yet eight o'clock, and there is no one in the streets. Dear Madame Bienfait, let me at least do your housework. I can wash the dishes, go and get water as I did at Escaladios, I can sweep, I will do all indeed. I will be the little servant, and you will be the lady. So you will not be so tired, and you will have more time to sew; you will make more money, and Jean Paul will not bring you to poverty."

M. Bienfait patted him on his cheek and said, "You are a good boy!" Then he went out with his precious box under his arm.   Madeleine also went to her work at the mantua-maker's.

Jean Paul stayed with Mme. Bienfait until all was cleaned, and the room put in order, then he went down three times with a large jug to the fountain in the yard, and brought it up each time filled with water.   He wanted also to make the purchases for dinner, but Mme. Bienfait could not trust to any one the choice of the small piece of meat and the vegetables necessary for their evening meal.

"I entreat you," said Jean Paul, "to let me go in your place; I will beg the butcher so hard, and I will tell him how good you are that he will let me have everything cheap."

Mme. Bienfait would not yield; she went out with her basket on her arm.

Jean Paul was quite alone in his friend's chamber. What could he do?   It was only ten o'clock.   Jean Paul knew very well that in the forenoon there were only business people in the streets, who did not stop to look at anything that was shown them, and who gave nothing.   It was only in the afternoon that the little children went out, and the fine ladies walked.   What could he do, then?   Commonly, he went out to get his breakfast, sauntered along by the shops, and afterwards came in for his little mice; but to-day he did not desire to saunter.   Mme. Bienfait's room spoke of work—all there was in order, dusted, mended, cleaned, washed.   Jean Paul looked around him.   All at once, he saw on the mantelpiece his prayer book, and the famous story of Little Roger.   He did not feel much tempted to touch it.

"Bah!" said he, "it is not amusing, but Madeleine will be so pleased."

And now he has taken up the two books, he searches, he compares, he counts—and oh! what good luck! he has found the ten famous *Ours!* "There is *Father*, there are only six of them. But the *whos!* see them, see them! How glad and astonished Madeleine will be this evening!" He intends to do the same every day.

Meanwhile, Jean Paul had applied himself so much, that his cheeks were burning, and the little words danced before his eyes. He put the books back again on the mantelpiece.

Mme. Bienfait came back. The sun was shining brightly; it came down into the yard. The water that he had got for Mme. Bienfait reminded him that Madeleine had told him that fountains were not made for poodles. He did not dare to ask himself, either, what M. Bienfait thought of him; but since he was to dine now every day with his friends, he would never again forget this dear fountain, he would go there twice a day, he would be clean—clean as Madeleine's father.

At eight o'clock in the evening, when M. Bienfait and Madeleine came in, Jean Paul was there; he had set the table, he had blown the fire, and he was stirring the stew.

"Our affair gets along nicely," said M. Bienfait at dinner-time. "I reached Monsieur Aubersart's just as he was going out, but he took the time to listen to all my story, all your story, Jean Paul. He is so good, you would have thought he took pleasure in hearing about the mice, and about your mother. I was going to ask him what was to be done to get back your money, but I had not that trouble. He took the little paper from my hands which I had just read to him and on which I had written how your famous bag was made. He smiled while reading it:

" 'That will do, father Bienfait,' said he, 'I am going to write to Bordeaux; I will take charge of this little affair. Come back—let me see—in two weeks, I think you will find here the little bag worked with red cotton.'

"I thanked him very much. He told me, with his kind smile, that he was glad to do me a service, as well as the little master of the mice, and I went away very joyful. You see that it is just the same now, as if you had your bag of money in your hands."

Jean Paul would have liked to thank the good M. Bienfait, but his mouth was so full he could not say a word; and when he had swallowed his big potato, and he wanted to speak, his heart was so full of gratitude that it choked him. He saw himself, he, the poor, forsaken one, received as a beloved child; he had found a father, mother, and a sister. The tears came into his eyes.

"Oh," said he, "you are all, you are always good to Jean Paul from morning till night."

Madeleine sent him a kiss, and Mme. Bienfait said some affectionate words to him, and patted his cheek; then she changed the conversation—she saw the emotion of the poor little boy, and did not wish to increase it.

In the evening pupil and mistress were enchanted with each other. Madeleine found that Jean Paul had made so much progress that she went for her slate, and began to make him write the first words that he read so well.

"It is more amusing to write than to read," said Jean Paul.

The mistress and pupil would perhaps have gone on with their lesson all night, if at ten o'clock Mme. Bienfait had not sent them to bed.

Chapter XXIV

Jean Paul no longer has a secretary

THEY were at dinner again some days afterwards. Jean Paul passed his plate to Madeleine, who held it out to M. Bienfait. It was M. Bienfait who helped the soup; but when his plate came back, instead of the soup, Jean Paul found—What? the little bag! yes, the little yellow bag with the red letters. He opened it and counted. There was only one piece missing—it still contained fourteen francs! Jean Paul jumped from his chair, clapped his hands, and sang out with joy. He would have forgotten his soup if M. Bienfait and Madeleine had not thought of it, and filled a plate of it for him.

"But it is not two weeks," said Jean Paul, "since that good gentleman told you to come for the bag."

"Two weeks to-day," answered M. Bienfait.

"How good you are to have thought of it!" said Jean Paul. "I had forgotten it. How quickly the time has passed!"

Jean Paul was right; those two weeks had passed very fast. He had learned his lessons well, he had studied zealously; all were pleased with him. Two weeks pass very quickly when one is busily employed.

That evening, our friend did such wonders on his slate, that Madeleine declared that he knew how to make all his letters.

INSTEAD OF THE SOUP, JEAN PAUL FOUND—

"All, all?" asked Jean Paul.

"Yes, all," answered Madeleine.

"Then," said Jean Paul, "I know how to write."

"Yes, you are beginning," replied Madeleine. "I have thought of something!" said she immediately.

She spoke in a low voice to Jean Paul, who answered in the same tone; a minute after, she got up, and went to the bureau, and took from it many things which she wanted; then the two children seemed to be engaged in some terrible work. Madeleine was leaning towards Jean Paul and seemed at the same time to be encouraging and correcting him, but always in a low voice. Jean Paul bent over the table, and was quite silent. M. and Mme. Bienfait asked one another what this great affair could be, which was giving them so much trouble. At last, after a long hour, Madeleine cried out "Victory! Victory! Mother, father! Jean Paul has written to his mother!"

And she showed them triumphantly a sheet of letter paper, on which was written in letters as big as a finger, rather shaky, rather crooked, a little humpbacked, but very easily read, these few words:

"Darling mother, Jean Paul loves you; here are fourteen francs."

"Why!" said Mme. Bienfait, "It can be read very well—it is really well written."

"You understand, mamma," Madeleine explained, "we have only written what was necessary. Jean Paul wanted to write about my father, about you, the mice, and his sisters, and so on. But my poor Jean Paul, we would have been a month writing a letter like that. Think, father! he was obliged to write letter by letter."

M. Bienfait laughed. "Oh, I know well, my dear, that you are an excellent teacher." He looked at the letter. "Really, it is not badly done at all; only Jean Paul must sign it, so that his mother may see that it was he who had written it."

"Oh, darling father!" Madeleine counted on her fingers. "Eight letters yet to write! J-e-a-n P-a-u-l. It will take us at least twenty minutes to do it. And we are so tired! and it is already ten o'clock. Little father, have the goodness to add in your good handwriting, 'It was Jean Paul who wrote this.' Afterwards you can write the address, and put the money in the letter, father, as you did last time; you can do all that so well! then your little Madeleine will kiss you, and thank you, and go to bed."

"And Jean Paul, also, if you please."

The good M. Bienfait added the few words, folded the letter, wrote the address, and sent it off the next day to Escaladios.

But as soon as the good father came in to his dinner, Madeleine ran to him.

"Father," said she, "the letter! have you put the letter in the post?"

"Certainly," said M. Bienfait, "very early this morning. Did not my dear little daughter tell me to do so?" said he, kissing her.

"Would you be able to get it back again?"

"Impossible, my child, it is on its way to Escaladios, and already perhaps it is half-way there."

"What a pity! father, two weeks ago Jean Paul gave two francs and fifty centimes to mamma, to keep for him, and we have forgotten to put them with the fourteen francs from Bordeaux which have gone to his mother. I have just found them in the little box, while I was putting the drawer in order."

"But I did not forget them at all, Mademoiselle Madeleine," said her mother. "I knew perfectly where they were."

"Then, mamma, why did you not give them to us yesterday, when Jean Paul wrote his letter?"

"I kept them to buy shoes for our friend, who would soon be barefoot; when he makes as much more, he will have a nice pair of new shoes."

"How well it was to do so, my little mother! But then you always do right. But poor Jean Paul also wants a new blouse."

"I will see to the blouse." She glanced at her husband, laughing.

And he said, mischievously, "You say you will see to Jean Paul's blouse—I don't know whether that is so—but you are seeing to mine pretty sharply, at any rate." She laughed.

"I have a project in my head," went on Mme. Bienfait, still laughing. "Just look husband, the sleeves, the upper part of the back, the front are all worn out. This blouse that you wear is worth nothing, but it will make a fine one for Jean Paul."

"Then, my wife, this blouse does not belong to me— and I am wearing Jean Paul's blouse. That doesn't seem right. I shall be afraid to wear it. If I take it off while I am at dinner, it will be safer. What do you say about it, Jean Paul?" He pretended to take off his blouse.

Jean Paul and Madeleine ran toward him.   "Oh! father!"   "Oh! Monsieur Bienfait!"

"Well, I will wear it, since you permit me, and thank you.   Can I wear it a few days longer?   I will promise to do all that I can to keep it clean.   I will try not to be burned or drowned."

Mme. Bienfait and Madeleine cried together, "Oh! don't speak of that even in fun!"

Then they sat down to table and dined gaily.

Chapter XXV

The Tuileries.   The presentation

THE summer had come.   There was neither cold,
nor rain, nor mud now.   The air was warm; the
pavement was white and dusty; and what was seen of
the sky between the high houses of the faubourg Saint
Marceau was of a bright blue.

When Jean Paul heard them say that the summer was here, he made them repeat it—then he sighed. The summer for him was large trees bending under their weight of leaves and flowers, the sweet-smelling linden trees, the grass of the meadows hid under the blue flowers of the gentian, and the June sun making the snow shine on the high mountains.

In Mme. Bienfait's room they did not sew in the evening around the table. And there were no more reading lessons by the light of the lamp, for Jean Paul had learned very quickly. As soon as our friends had finished their dinner, they went out to breathe a little fresh air. Mme. Bienfait's room was small, but still they were obliged to light the fire to cook the dinner; and so our friends, big and little, were nearly stifled there, and hurried with their dinner, that they might go out the sooner.

Sometimes, when the weather was fine, they took very long walks. They wanted to see the trees dressed in their summer attire, to be sure that the earth could produce something else besides the high white houses of their gloomy faubourg.

One evening, the heat was stifling. Jean Paul, Madeleine, M. and Mme. Bienfait went as far as the Tuileries. Madeleine, her father and mother were delighted to sit down under the big chestnut trees. Jean Paul would have liked very much to have sat down beside them, and to have talked to his dear Madeleine, but he had brought his little theatre and his actresses, and he wanted to try to give some performances by the lights from the shops. He left his friends, promising them to return soon to join them.

"Take notice where we are," said Madeleine to him. "It is the first bench under the trees, beside the large reservoir."

"Yes, yes," answered Jean Paul.

"And you know they shut the gates at ten o'clock," said M. Bienfait in his turn.

"Oh, I will be back again long before ten o'clock," answered Jean Paul, as he went away.

Oh! how pleasant it was under those big chestnut trees!

Nevertheless, more than one fine lady passed near our friends, and they heard them say that the public gardens were odious, that you could breathe nothing but dust there; and in a heat like this, the Bois de Boulogne was the only supportable place.

Our three friends had been shut up all day. M. Bienfait in the locksmith's shop, Madeleine at the mantua-maker's, and Mme. Bienfait in her room. They had all borne the heat and burden of the day, so the rest and recreation seemed to them delicious. The night was coming on, a little breeze sprang up, moving the leaves, and cooling the foreheads of the child and her parents. All three of them were quite happy to be together, each one happy in seeing the others happy. They did not look at the gaily dressed crowd that filled the wide walks—they looked at the rose-colored clouds, and at the stars which showed themselves gradually as the darkness increased.

"They do their duty," M. Bienfait was saying to himself. "Everything in the world obeys God—sun, stars and trees—man alone is disobedient. Oh, my heavenly Father! I want to obey Thee in all things, and always."

And Mme. Bienfait was saying to herself:

"How beautiful the world is! How good He is, Who has made our place of trial so beautiful! We are only birds of passage. Life, it is said, is but a journey which leads us to heaven! How good He is Who made our pathway so pleasant! And what will Paradise be— Our Father's house!"

Madeleine was thinking of Escaladios, of Jean Paul's mother, and his little sisters, of whom they were talking while walking here.

But suddenly, "Ran, ran, ran tan plan!"

"Now we must leave," said M. Bienfait.

"What! already?" said Mme. Bienfait. "It is not ten o'clock."

"There, it is striking now," said M. Bienfait; "they are going to shut the gates."

"And Jean Paul!" cried Madeleine.

"They are shutting up!" cried one of the keepers of the garden.

Everybody had gone out excepting a few persons who were belated as they were, and whom the keepers drove towards the gates.

Our friends looked all around them, and tried to see through the darkness—no sign of Jean Paul!

"It is distressing!" said Madeleine. "How will he find his way in the dark?"

"Do not worry yourself," said M. Bienfait. "Jean Paul is more than two years old."

At last they passed through the gate.

"There he is! there he is!" cried Madeleine.

And indeed Jean Paul was there talking to the sentry, who would not let him go in. Jean Paul insisted upon going in because his friends were waiting for him on the bench, near the reservoir; he was beginning to be very angry. Fortunately, Madeleine's arm rubbed against his arm; he turned around, recognized his friends, and only thought of the joy of finding them again.

"How late you are!" said Madeleine, with a slight tone of reproval.

"It was not my fault; I was not able to come back sooner—I will tell you all about it. I am very much pleased."

Madeleine asked quickly, "Have you made much money?"

"Not a sou."

Madeleine was disappointed. "You are not hard to please, if you are satisfied!"

"Listen, listen—you'll see."

"The first thing I want to know, is where you have been?"

Jean Paul said, "I crossed the great place with statues——"

Madeleine interrupted, "The place de la Concorde."

Jean Paul went on: "Then it seemed to me it was light, very light, a little farther on, at the beginning of a wide street——"

"The rue Royale."

"So I went in that direction. There was a large shop full of gilded chandeliers all lighted, and it was brighter than midday—only what were all these bright lights for? There was nobody in the shop, but a

woman seated on a kind of throne. This woman must
have liked to see everything clearly, as she had all this
lighted up for herself! and then outside on the pavement, there were a great many little round tables, and
a number of gentlemen, ladies, and even children,
seated around these tables. All were eating pretty red
and white things, and drinking sparkling drinks."

"In a word, it was a café, we know what that is—
go on."

"And then much further on than the pavement, a
great many handsome carriages were standing! you
know, Madeleine, those carriages which look like bas-
kets and the ladies in them look as if they were lying
down."

"An open calèche,—go on!"

"And then, in all these carriages, they ate the same
pretty red and white things."

"Yes, I know—go on, go on."

"You may be sure, that when I saw all these people,
I promised myself a famous harvest! Then I stole in
quietly, in the midst of these tables and chairs, to find a
little place for my theatre. But it was not so easy!
There were a great number of men bareheaded, with
large white aprons."

"The waiters!" said Madeleine, a little impatiently.

"Then the gentlemen were calling: 'Waiter, a strawberry ice! a decanter of ice water,' and I do not know
what else. The men with the big white aprons answered bawling: 'Coming! coming!' and they ran over
the pavement carrying waiters filled with good things.
They ran so fast that two or three times I was nearly
knocked over; meanwhile I had made myself as small

as possible, and had managed to place myself between two tables. I was quite near the glass wall of the shop, and I saw a handsome lady. Then I opened my little theatre. The chandeliers lighted it up brilliantly, it was perfect."

"Perfect! I should think so—and then?"

"Wait, you will see. I took my mice out of my little bag, and I commenced the performance. But bah! in the midst of such a noise, and in such a heat, and with so many good things to eat, who could pay attention to my lady, to Rosette, and to poor Jean Paul? They were talking, screaming, and laughing; nobody saw me. Yes, somebody saw me. It was one of the big men with white aprons. 'Wait, you vagabond,' said he to me, 'I am going to show you the way out of here. What! you see we have scarcely room to turn here, and you come to encumber us with all sorts of nasty beasts, beginning with yourself.' He came rapidly towards me; fortunately the tables kept him from passing, and obliged him to go around them. I hoped to have time to run away; suddenly I was seized by the shoulders, and shaken so violently, that I thought the theatre, my lady and Rosette were on the ground."

"Oh! how dreadful!" Madeleine trembled with fright. "Go on!"

"But they let me go. There stood before us a tall servant, with a petticoat so long, so long."

"Simply, a servant in livery—go on! and this servant?"

"He drew my persecutor towards him by the apron, and said, 'Madame the countess told me to ask you to send that child to her.' He pointed to me with his finger. 'Madame the countess!' answered the other, smiling most charmingly, 'with the greatest pleasure. Enchanted, really! I am going to take him to her myself; come, my child!' And he took my hand so gently, that I looked at him with all my eyes, in order to be sure that it was the same waiter who had treated me with so much rudeness an instant before. 'Where is Madame the Countess?' said he. The tall servant in the petticoat pointed out to us one of those little carriages, you know, Madeleine, that do not look like a basket, but are like a very little box."

"Yes, yes, I know; I believe they call them broughams; that is nothing, go on!"

"There was a little lady inside of it, very old; but very nice. Only think, her hair was as white as my lady's fur, only much longer. It was arranged prettily in puffs under her bonnet. My companion bowed down to the ground to her: 'Does Madame the Countess desire any refreshment?' said he, never leaving off smiling. 'I hurried to bring this young man, that I might obey the order of Madame the Countess. As the heat is so great, perhaps Madame will take an ice; the strawberry is excellent. Has any one waited upon Madame the Countess?' he cried to the waiters who passed.

" 'Thank you, Monsieur Eugène,' answered a very feeble but very sweet voice from the inside of the carriage, 'I will take nothing this evening. My husband went into the café to order fifty little ices for tomorrow, and I am waiting for him. I beg you to see that they are good, Monsieur Eugène; they are for children. Take care not to put anything in them that would hurt them.'

"'Do not be uneasy, Madame the Countess,' M. Eugène answered, smiling. 'They shall be perfect, exquisite; we are always enchanted to have the honor of supplying Madame the Countess. Oh! here is Monsieur the Count!' said he, turning himself around, and bowing again to the ground.

"A tall old man drew near the carriage, leaning on his cane. Madeleine, I cannot tell you how it was; he made me feel afraid, and at the same time, I should have liked to kiss him, he looked so very good. He stooped a little, as if, from his goodness, he wanted to draw near to you.

"'I have just written your order myself, my dear,' said he to the little lady. 'You may be easy on that subject, it will be well done.'

"'And I, while I was waiting for you, gave my instructions to Monsieur Eugène,' she answered smiling.

"M. Eugène took advantage of this to relate to them I do not know what—that he was going to be the owner of the café, and he begged the Count not to withdraw his patronage, and so on.

"During this time, my dear old gentleman had got into the carriage and was seated alongside of the little lady.

"'Shall we go home now?' said he to her. He leaned out of the carriage window to give his orders to the servant in a petticoat.

"I was still there wondering why the little lady had called me but not daring to speak.

"'Wait a minute! a minute!' said she, quickly. 'A

little while ago, while you were in the café, I——'
Then do you see, Madeleine it was in vain to listen, she
spoke so low that I heard nothing more. However, I
did not dare to go away; perhaps she was speaking of
me.

"After a few minutes, the gentleman put his head
out of the carriage door.

" 'Where is the little boy who shows the mice?' said
he.

" 'Here I am, my good sir !'

" 'Very well, my child. Will you come to-morrow
at eight o'clock with your little mice in their handsomest
dresses to gain a nice five-franc piece; *rue* —— *rue*
——?' he said to me. How does it happen that I have
forgotten it?"

"Now you have spoiled all! you have forgotten it !"

"Rue— what was it? number ten or six."

How frightened Madeleine was now. "Number ten
or six !"

Jean Paul said slowly, "It is a street that has not at
all a funny name. What is it then?"

"Try and remember."

"Rue—ah, the little lady said right, when she said I
would forget it."

"You should have begged her to repeat it to you,"
said Madeleine in despair.

"I did not dare to, for all at once, she put on her
spectacles, and took a little book from her pocket, tore
a leaf from it and wrote upon it; then she gave it to
me and the coachman started off."

"And have you lost this little paper?"

"No, no, here it is."

"Why did you not say so?" cried Madeleine in great relief. "What difference did it make if you had forgotten the address?"

"How could I read it in the dark? And I thought you wanted to know at once where I was to go tomorrow."

"Oh! we will have plenty of time to see that at home. But here we are. The story you have told me has made the way seem very short."

Indeed, they had now arrived before their old house. M. and Mme. Bienfait said good evening to Mme. Fumeron and her husband, who were taking the air at the entrance of the porte-cochère, but Jean Paul did not dare to say a word to the good portress.

In spite of the darkness, he imagined that he saw M. Fumeron frowning, and motioning for him to pass along quickly.

"And yet I pay him my rent every two weeks. I have never failed to do so," he said very low to Madeleine, drawing her into the yard.

The two children ran quickly up the long staircase; Madeleine had the key of her mother's chamber; she opened it quickly, looked for the match-box, took the candle, lighted it, and when M. and Mme. Bienfait came into the room, she was reading a little paper aloud.

"To-morrow Thursday, at eight o'clock, rue de la Paix, No. 15, ask for the Count de Tourlaville."

Madeleine and Jean Paul soon explained to the dear parents where this precious paper had come from. Then they kissed each other and they separated until the next day.

CHAPTER XXVI

Jean Paul goes into the fashionable world

THE next day Madeleine hurried to return to her mother's. She had asked permission to leave the workroom a little earlier than usual, and wanted to arrive at home before Jean Paul started. It was a little after seven o'clock when, on going up the stairs, she met on the second story Jean Paul coming down.

"Good evening, Madelichon. Oh! how tired you look, how red you are!"

"I was hoping to arrive before you started, my little Jean Paul, I believe I have run every step of the way. Let me see. How are you dressed?"

She made him go back a few steps before the window, that she might examine him.

"Let me see, have you your white shirt on? your new blouse? your nice shoes? very well, let's see." She hesitated. "Let's see this dear fat face and these hands. White as snow; your hair nicely combed! My dear Jean Paul, you are superb! And let us look also at the mice. Oh, how it would have amused me to have dressed them. Stop, I forgot! I brought you a long sash of black silk to put over my lady's sacque. I made it in the workroom, during luncheon time; it is the last fashion, you know! There, how nicely it fits her, and how well it shows her figure."

"Thank you, darling Madelichon," said Jean Paul, "and good-bye, I have only time to take my long walk to the rue de la Paix, and to be there at eight o'clock!"

"You know the way, I hope?"

"Oh, thank you!" answered he, while going down the steps, "your good mother has explained it well to me, it was she also who made me put on my new blouse, and my white shirt; good-bye, Madeleine! How I wish that you could go with me! but your mamma says it is impossible."

"It would have amused me very much," said Madeleine sighing, then she ran lightly up the staircase, crying out,

"Good-bye, little Jean Paul, go quickly; good luck!" Jean Paul reached the rue de la Paix. He rang at a fine large door. The door opened, he entered into a magnificent vaulted courtyard, quite filled with flowers. The porter's lodge seemed to him so beautiful, that he thought at first the Count de Tourlaville lived there. Fortunately our Jean Paul knew how to read, and he saw written in golden letters above the glass door of this handsome parlor, "Concierge." He hesitated, however, to disturb this fat gentleman whom he saw extended full length in a nice armchair, reading the newspaper.

"He is so different from Monsieur Fumeron, that he can't be a porter," said our friend to himself.

While Jean Paul was hesitating, some one came in by the street door. He was an elegant young man. He shut the outside door violently, and ran towards the concierge's lodge, and without paying any attention to the reader of the newspaper, he cried out,

"The Count de Tourlaville, if you please?"

"On the second floor; the staircase fronts you," answered the fat man, without disturbing himself.

"Very well," said Jean Paul, "I have only to follow this gentleman, and I shall be sure to arrive directly at Monsieur Tourlaville's rooms." He crossed the vestibule decorated with flowers, and went up two or three steps on the thickest of carpets.

"How nice this is!" thought he. "So there are staircases with velvet steps. If Madeleine were here!"

"Well! where are you going?" a rough voice cried to him from the bottom of the staircase.

Jean Paul, lost in admiration, did not even know it was to him that this question was addressed.

"Well, where are you going? You, I mean, you boy in the blouse!" cried the voice, still more roughly than before, and at the same time, that Jean Paul might know that it was to him the man was speaking, a rough hand seized hold of him by the arm.

"I am going to the Count de Tourlaville's in the second story, as this gentleman is doing," he answered.

"Yes, indeed! as this gentleman is doing! Then such blackguards as you are to use fine staircases and carpets! Just look at your feet; the street has just been watered, and every step of this little rascal has left a mark on the carpet! Get out, you beggar!"

"But I did not know that this was made not to walk upon. I only followed this gentleman," said Jean Paul.

"What a stupid little beast you are!" said the concierge. "He does not seem to understand that the handsome staircase is made for gentlefolks, and the servants' staircase for him. Go to the end of the yard

Jean Paul and Madeleine

opposite to you," he cried, pushing Jean Paul at the same time with his strong hand into the yard.

"There are fine houses, and ugly ones, but the concierges are the same everywhere!" Jean Paul said to himself, thinking again of M. Fumeron.

He felt much more at home on the small staircase, a little dirty, and very steep, that the concierge had pointed out to him. He felt so much at home, that he went up, went up, until he arrived at the sixth story.

"Why, I am crazy!" he said to himself, as he found himself opposite a very dirty closet, the door of which was wide open. "I thought I was at home. It is to the second story that I am to go; how am I to know it again? That will be very hard to do in going down. I had better go quite down to the bottom of the staircase, and then go up again attentively."

Our little friend did this. He went down the six stories, then ran up two; fortunately he was not very heavy and he remembered the proverb, "Use your head to save your heels."

Quite out of breath, he knocked at a little door. It was opened for him. He went into the kitchen, but he had not time to look about him. They seemed to expect him. He had hardly said "The Count de Tourlaville," when a servant beckoned him to follow him; which Jean Paul obeyed.

"This way, this way," said the servant, while crossing the large kitchen, and then a long entry.

He opened a door, made Jean Paul go before him, and then shut it.

He had scarcely entered, when he was obliged to lean against the wall, and put his hands before his dazzled eyes.   He was in a large saloon all covered with gold, filled with chandeliers, and lighted with wax candles. He heard lively and joyous music, and he saw through his fingers a crowd of children, who were dancing to the sound of it.   It seemed to Jean Paul as if he were dreaming.   It seemed to him that he was in fairyland, when he saw all these little curly heads, all these little embroidered skirts turning round, and the long ribbons which floated in the air, all those sturdy little legs, and little feet which moved in time or out of time, but above all, those dear little faces, those little open mouths, those laughs which made music of another kind but still sweeter.   All this was for him a fairy world.

Meanwhile, the music stopped; the little army of dancers were broken up.   They could be seen going, coming, swarming in different parts of the saloon. Some of the children came near Jean Paul and looked at him silently.   Our poor friend did not dare to move; he was quite abashed; he felt that he was blushing like a peony; his eyes were still covered with his hands; he felt that they were looking at him, that everybody was looking at him; he was ready to cry.   He would have liked to hide himself under the table, in the chimney place or anywhere.

"Well! where is he?" said a voice mildly and quietly, and which Jean Paul thought he recognized.   "I gave orders that he was to come to my son's room, and I was told that he was in the saloon.   Ah! there he is, my little friend."

Jean Paul, still looking through his fingers, saw

approaching the good gentleman that he had seen the night before.

"Make room!" said he, dispersing the children who surrounded Jean Paul. "Make room for grandfather!"

"Grandfather," said the fattest, the freshest, and the curliest of the little boys of five years of age, "grandfather, are we to have the surprise now?"

"Yes, if you are very good, if you all go to the other end of the drawing-room, and turn your backs, do you hear? Run off! go!"

All the little feet began to run, and soon nothing could be seen but little dimpled backs, little rosy calves, and little heels stamping impatiently.

In the meantime, the old gentleman had first chucked Jean Paul under the chin, then softly removed his hand from his eyes.

"Do not be afraid, my child," said he to him. "We are very glad to see you here, and we are sure that you will amuse us very much."

"Yes, yes," said the little lady, who also came near Jean Paul. "His little animals are wonderful. Do not be afraid, my friend, and in a few moments you will hear cries of admiration from these dear children."

These kind words reassured Jean Paul a little. He stooped down behind the good little lady and took his little actresses from his bag; then he placed them on the large card table in the middle of the room, which the old gentleman had just told them to open.

"Now you can come back, children, and place yourselves around the table, the smallest in front," said the good grandfather.

What a performance! what a success, what applause, what a stamping of feet amongst the lookers-on! The mothers and fathers, although not so demonstrative as the little ones, were very much amused.

Suddenly, without any one noticing him, the good papa rang the bell near the fireplace, then said a word in Jean Paul's ear.

"Hop! hop!" said Jean Paul.

Then the little mice ran into his arms, and afterwards hid themselves in their bag.

"Ah-ah-ah!" All the little mouths gave one cry of regret.

But just at that instant, the door opened and a great many servants came in, carrying trays filled with little plates. Each one seemed to contain a small fruit—it was ice cream.

"Oh! father, you are always the same, always too good," said a young man who approached the old gentleman.

"Yes," added a young lady, taking him by his hand, "my dear father-in-law knows how to make children happy. I had promised these little monkeys only cake and syrup, and here we have a grand entertainment, thanks to you, dear father—and dear mother," she added, taking the hand of the old lady.

"Ah!" answered the grandfather, "the ices were my idea, but the mice were your mother's thought; you must give her the credit of it."

The good grandmother smiled, then she chose a pretty rose-colored ice and gave it to Jean Paul, who was standing modestly in a corner of the room.

WHAT A PERFORMANCE!

209

"Well!" said she, after a moment's silence, "you do not eat your ice—it will melt."

"This will melt, then?" cried our friend. "And I wanted to keep it for Madeleine!"

He had to eat it; and we must confess that Jean Paul, who at first thought that it burned him, found it delicious.

Meanwhile all the little plates were empty; the mammas had wiped all the little mouths, and had sighed on seeing that more than one dress had been stained by the pretty ices. The old gentleman approached Jean Paul, and again whispered in his ear.

"Certainly, Monsieur," answered our friend.

And then a second performance began, which succeeded as well as the first, and was received with the same applause. The mice were at their last dance; but before Jean Paul had time to say, "Hop! hop!" and they to jump into his arms, the music began, and a pretty polka was played. Then the card table was folded and taken away as if by enchantment, and all the little children commenced dancing, jumping, and turning round.

The Count de Tourlaville took Jean Paul to the door of the drawing-room which led into the dining-room.

"Take care of this child," said he to the servant, who was there. "Give him a piece of brioche and a glass of syrup before he goes away."

Then stooping to Jean Paul, he said: "Here, my friend, this is what I promised you; your little animals are charming; you have amused the children very much."

Then he put a five-franc piece in his hand.

Jean Paul thanked the good gentleman, thanked the servant, and stood up near the round table to eat his brioche and drink his syrup.

Suddenly, he heard some one call.

"Constant! Constant! the Count is calling you to bring more ices."

"Coming! I'm coming!" said the servant, and ran out of the dining-room.

Jean Paul was not alone: a little man five years old, had glided into the room and stood up before him without speaking. Jean Paul recognized the grandson of the Count by his large hazel eyes, and his fair curling hair, which hid his neck and a part of his face. The child remained there standing motionless, his head bent, and his large eyes raised to Jean Paul.

Suddenly he shook back his curls, and raised his head.

"Give me the little mouse," he said in a firm voice.

"What do you say, my little sir?" answered Jean Paul, who thought he had not understood him.

"I said *give—me—the—little—mouse.*"

"Oh! impossible, my little gentleman," said Jean Paul, laughing.

"Yes, the one with the red dress; I will have it! I say I will!"

"Oh my little gentleman, really I cannot give it to you. I gain my own and my mother's livelihood by showing her."

"Oh, yes you can," answered the child, shaking his curls again from his face. "I'll explain it to you; you see to-day is my birthday. You understand? Everybody gives me anything I want; you see, grandpa has

given me a surprise; grandma, ice cream; and mamma
has made all my little friends come here in their pretty
white dresses. You understand. I tell you, give me
that little white mouse, my lady."

He held out his little hand, and seeing that Jean Paul
only answered by turning away his head,

"Come," said he, stamping his little foot on the floor,
"you don't understand then. You know very well that
they never refuse anything to children on their birthday."

"Ah! dear little gentleman!" answered Jean Paul,
sighing, "there are a great many little children who
have no birthday celebration at all."

"Oh that is not true! You say that only so as not to
give the mouse! But I, I know what I say is true.
All little children have their birthdays. I know it well
and all the little children do not have their birthdays
to-day." And he began to smile. "Give me the mouse,
I beg you. But you, when does your birthday come?
Tell me."

Jean Paul said sadly. "My birthday! mine! Oh,
dear little sir, I have never had my birthday celebrated."

The child was astonished. "Why? But that is not
possible! What is your name then? But then you
have no name!"

"My name is Jean Paul."

"Jean Paul!" He clapped his little hands. "Oh!
but this is your birthday, if your name is Jean. This
is Saint Jean's day." He jumped. "I know very well
that this is Saint Jean's day, it comes in the month of
June. Tell me what you have had given to you. Tell
me all! all!"

Jean Paul smiled. "Oh! but you see I have no good grandfather or grandmother to celebrate my birthday— my father's dead, and my mother is so poor that I send her all the money I make in showing my mice."

The little Jean spoke very sadly: "Then no one has given you anything on your birthday; you have had no presents or pretty playthings. I'm very sorry; I thought that——"

Jean Paul interrupted him: "You see now, my little gentleman, that I cannot give you my little mouse."

The little boy held his head down, and seemed to be thinking.

"Listen. Do you see, this is not fair! I have had for my birthday—oh, let me tell you: a box of chocolate, then a handsome horse, then money, then a whip, and then ices. I don't know what besides. You have had nothing at all! Do you see, that is not fair! I know what I will do: we must divide all between us. Since you are called Jean it is your birthday too." He moved forward into the dining-room. "But what shall I do? All my gifts are in mamma's room, and it is so dark there, I'm afraid to go there. You come with me."

"Thank you, my dear little gentleman, I do not want anything. If I only knew the way out!" Jean Paul went towards the door of the ante-chamber. The little Jean came to him and took hold of him.

"I want you to have some gifts for your birthday, Jean Paul." He searched in his pocket. "Oh, how lucky! Oh! here is my little box of chocolate; it is for you, and then my purse. You must take all the money that is in it. This way." He counted on his fingers. "I have the horse, and then the whip, and then you have the chocolate and the money. That is very well, isn't it?" He jumped with joy.

"But I will not take your little purse, nor your sugarplums," said Jean Paul.

The little Jean put the box of chocolate upon the table, opened it and put the purse in it. He raised himself on tiptoe, and pressed his little dimpled hands with all his strength on the cover of the box to shut it, then he put the box in Jean Paul's hands.

"I beg you to take it," said he, "it would make me very sorry, if you didn't. I beg you to take it."

The servant came back; Jean Paul wanted to explain it all to him, but the dear little fellow began to cry, and pulled Jean Paul towards the ante-chamber.

"I want him to go; I want him to go away at once," cried he, knowing very well that when Jean Paul had started he would not be able to return the box to any one. "Constant, make him go out, the bad boy, he has made me cry on my birthday."

"Who has made my dear little gentleman cry on his birthday?" said Constant, taking the child in his arms. "Yes, yes, we will both make him go away, the naughty fellow! away with you, sir."

Indeed, both of them opened the door and gently pushed Jean Paul out on the staircase, and he could neither make himself heard nor give one word of explanation. The little boy made so much noise, Jean Paul's voice could not be heard.

Chapter XXVII

Jean Paul makes a present

IN the meanwhile, Jean Paul had gone down a few steps—then he stopped, and reflected.

"What is to be done," he said to himself. "I will not, I ought not to take these sugarplums and this money from this dear little boy; no one has given him permission to give them to me. What is to be done? I will ring, and give back the box to the servant who opens the door for me. But if it should be Constant, and if the little Jean should be still there! No, it would be better for me to go down, and explain how it happened to the concierge, and leave the box with him; to-morrow he will give it back. Go down! ah! I am now on the horrid staircase of velvet, which was not made for me! What is to be done? I hear the concierge's voice, he is coming up—where shall I hide?"

Our friend had noticed alongside of him, in an arch of the window, a large china vase which contained one of those beautiful shrubs, with thick and glossy leaves. He slipped quickly behind it.

He was just in time! The big concierge had come there to attend to the gas, and was quite near Jean Paul.

At last, it is done; the concierge went down. Jean Paul breathed again, he listened, he heard the door shutting at the bottom of the staircase. He thought he would be able to come out of his hiding place, and he determined to ring at M. Tourlaville's door.

But he had hardly left his hiding place when he went back to it quickly. He heard a door open, then a sound of voices, and of good-byes, and of kisses, and laughs, and then again more good-byes, and at last the door was shut.

Jean Paul saw two persons coming down the staircase slowly. They took hold of the balustrade, and were coming near him. In front was a little old lady, and behind her—behind her—Yes! it was the good grandfather. Jean Paul is sure of it, he has recognized him.

So, the moment the old gentleman was going to pass by the shrub, Jean Paul ran out to meet him.

"Oh! if you please, monsieur—" said he.

The grandfather started—he was quite shaken by this sudden apparition.

"What is it? What is the matter?" said he, starting back a few steps. "Ah! it is the little mouse-boy! What do you want, my child?" added he, frowning. "Are you not satisfied with your evening?"

"My good sir, I want nothing; on the contrary, I want to give this back to you."

And he held out to him the little box of chocolate, and the little purse which was partly out of it.

"Why, it is the little blue purse that I gave Jean to-day!" cried the lady, who had come near them. "How did it get into your hands?"

"Unfortunate child!" cried the grandfather, sighing deeply, and taking the box and the purse from Jean Paul's hands. "You have then—found it? Where? how?"

"Dear good monsieur, I have neither stolen nor

found it," said Jean Paul, ready to cry, "it was your dear little boy who would positively give it to me, because he insisted that it was my birthday."

And Jean Paul related to the grandparents all that the child had said to him, and that after he had given him his purse, and his bonbons, the little man had pushed him out of the door to be quite sure that he would carry them away with him.

"But, dear monsieur," said Jean Paul, when he had finished, "I would not take advantage of the goodness of heart of this dear little fellow to rob him. To-morrow, please give him back his money and bonbons, and tell his father and mother that he is good as an angel."

The old gentleman and lady did not answer; they drew near to each other, and took each other's hands. Jean Paul saw the two clasped hands tremble, and he did not dare to break the silence.

At last the old gentleman said in a low voice, "You are an honest boy, my child."

Then he put the purse and box in his hand.

"Keep them," said he. "God forbid that I should undo the good action of my little grandson! No, I will never give him back this purse, or these bonbons, and I will never even speak to him of them; I wish that his first good act may remain a secret between him and the good God. O God, I thank Thee; make him love more and more every day those who suffer!"

The good grandfather was silent; Jean Paul thought he was praying.

"My boy," the little lady suddenly said in an agitated voice, "will you make me a present?"

"Oh! madame, with all my heart!" answered Jean Paul.

"Well, keep the money which is in the purse that Jean forced you to take, and give me the empty purse; it will be a souvenir of the first good act of my grandson. Put your money into this sugarplum box, so that you may not lose it."

She took from her pocket quite a small box that she gave to Jean Paul. He emptied the blue porte-monnaie into it, and handed it to the old lady, who kissed it, and held it in her hand.

"Thank you, my child!" said she to him. "You have made us very happy. Be all your life an honest man."

The three went down together, Jean Paul following the two old people. Jean Paul had no fear, he felt he was protected. They crossed the vestibule silently. But when the porte-cochère was shut behind him, Jean Paul turned towards the house.

"Thank you, dear little Monsieur Jean," cried he with all his might, "you ought to know at least that Jean Paul is grateful."

"Thank you, Monsieur Grandpapa, and Madame Grandmamma, you are all good people!" cried he again, on seeing the little carriage go away, which the Count and Countess had just got into.

Then our friend Jean Paul danced a mountain dance on the pavement, as if to give vent to the joy that had nearly stifled him. The passers-by began to assemble around him, so he took to his heels and ran home.

An hour afterwards, lying on his bundle of straw, he fell asleep smiling.

Chapter XXVIII

Other gifts from Jean Paul

THE next morning at Mme. Bienfait's they spoke only of little Jean.

Jean Paul came early into his friend's room, and put on the table the box of chocolate, the sugarplum box, and the five-franc piece.

"Look, Madelichon, I brought all this back last evening," said he.

"Let me see them," said Madeleine, running to the table. "First of all, a nice five-franc piece for your mother; that is the best."

"No, it isn't," said Jean Paul, laughing.

"Next," continued Madeleine, as she opened the box, "some chocolate sugarplums. Look! Look! Why, this is very nice, Monsieur Jean Paul."

"Go on still," said Jean Paul.

"And," continued the little girl, opening with great care the sugarplum box, "real gold pieces—one of ten francs, and two of five francs."

"Is it possible? So much as that?" cried Jean Paul. "What good luck!"

"You did not know then what was in the little box?" asked Madeleine.

"I knew very well that there was money in it, but as I always do, I wanted you to have the pleasure of counting it the first, Mademoiselle Madeleine. And how much does that make?"

"Five and five make ten, and then ten make twenty, and that, with the big piece, will make twenty-five francs for your mother!" cried Madeleine.

"Are you quite sure? so much as that?" asked Jean Paul.

"Yes, ask mamma if it isn't so," said Madeleine. "But who has given you all this money?"

"Come to breakfast," said Mme. Bienfait, "the coffee and milk are hot."

While eating, Jean Paul told them all that had happened the night before. Madeleine listened so attentively, that she forgot to eat her breakfast. When Jean Paul told them how the little Jean had insisted upon his giving him the lady mouse:

"You did not give it to him, I hope?" cried Madeleine. "That little Jean is a real spoiled child. To ask you for my lady!"

"Do not be afraid, Madeleine; my lady is sleeping peacefully in my room," answered Jean Paul. "But wait a little while before you judge my little Jean. You shall soon know more about him."

And Jean Paul went on with his story.

"Well," said he, when he had done, "is my little Jean spoiled?"

"A little—for all that," answered Madeleine, smiling.

"Come," began Mme. Bienfait, who saw that Jean Paul was quite sad at hearing his benefactor spoken of in this way, "if they spoil this dear child a little, it it because he is so good, and they love him so much."

"That's it," said Jean Paul, "and now let us make

a division; this pretty little sugarplum box is for you, Madame Bienfait, the box of chocolate is for you, Madeleine, and the twenty-five francs are for my mother."

"And my father, he has nothing!" said Madeleine. "Jean Paul, my friend, this is not fair, as little Jean would say. You must go back and take some more lessons from him. I am going to show you how to be fair."

She took from the bureau an old copy book, tore two leaves from it, made two cornucopias in which she emptied all the pastilles of chocolate, then shut the empty box.

"Now, Monsieur Jean Paul, begin your distribution again, if you please. The sugarplum box for mamma, that's well; the beautiful white and gold box for father, who can put his pens, wafers, and all sorts of things in it; a cornucopia for Madeleine, and one for Jean Paul. And now I have taught you how to make a fair division."

Jean Paul wanted her to take the two cornucopias, but she positively refused. He revenged himself upon her, by opening his, and making all his friends eat his sugarplums.

It was raining; a heavy June rain. M. Bienfait and Madeleine, protected by their umbrellas, went to their workshops. Jean Paul took his pen, and commenced writing to his mother. Oh! what joy to have such a large sum of money to send to her!

When the letter was finished and folded, he took it to Mme. Bienfait, and begged her to write the address, that it might be more easily read; then he asked her where the post-office was. Mme. Bienfait told him the nearest one, and advised him not to put either the money or the letter in the letter box but to go into the post-office and give it to one of the clerks.

Jean Paul set off; very glad to spare his good friend M. Bienfait the trouble of posting his letter.

"When we know how to read and write, we can attend to our own affairs without annoying our friends," said he to himself. And indeed Jean Paul executed this little affair very well; the letter and money reached his mother very safely, for a few days after, when he came home to dine with his friends, Madeleine threw her arms around his neck, and said,

"A letter, Jean Paul, a letter for you! It was I who brought it! Mamma was going to open it, but we saw that the address was 'Madame Bienfait, for Jean Paul.' Then we waited. Look! here it is!"

Jean Paul took the letter, and kissed it so hard and so often, that it was all rumpled.

"It must be from my mother," said he, and he kissed it again.

Then he tried to read the address, but he could not yet read handwriting very well.

"Then you don't want to know what's inside? Let us see! do open it!" said Madeleine.

Jean Paul tried to loosen the wafer.

"I am afraid of tearing it," said he to Madeleine. "Open it yourself, and read it to me."

"Let us make haste, then," said Madeleine. "Father will soon be home to dinner."

She sat down upon a chair near the open window, and Jean Paul sat down upon a stool at her feet.

"How happy I am!" he said.

"You might say, how happy we all are!" replied Madeleine. "I am as glad as you are, I am sure." And she began to read aloud.

Chapter XXIX

News from his own country and plans for the future

H IS mother began by thanking Jean Paul for the three letters he had written to her, and for all the money that he had sent her. She was very much astonished that her dear child had been able to earn so much. She feared that he had deprived himself of everything, in order to send her such large sums of money. She had not been able to write to him sooner, as all his little sisters had been sick one after the other. What would have become of them or of his mother, without the money from her good boy? For his mother had not been able to work much during the winter.

But now, all was going on well at Escaladios, said she. His little sisters were in perfect health, and M. Legras, who had come very often to the little house since Jean Paul had left, had taken a fancy to Louise. He had seen her take such good care of her little sister Marie, that he had asked her mother to let her come and help his wife to take care of their new-born babe; so that Louise was fed, clothed, and provided for in every way by Mme. Legras, and indeed was treated exactly as if she were her own child.

His mother told him also that his father's sister, a skilful mantua-maker at Bagnères-de-Bigorre, had come to Escaladios to see them, and that she had ad-

225

vised them very earnestly to come and work with her at Bagnères, where they had so much work during the bathing season.

"It is two days since we came to Bagnères," wrote his mother. "Your aunt is so kind to us, that although her house is very small, she has found room for us in it. You sisters and I sleep together in a very clean garret. In summer one can lodge very well anywhere. Angéle begins to work very nicely, and helps us very much. She sews and hems beautifully. The two children have gone to the Asylum, where they pass the day, and are learning to read.

"I could hardly make up my mind to go to Bagnères; my dear child, your aunt pressed us very much to go, and even offered to pay our expenses, but I still hesitated, for you must know, my dear boy, your sisters and I were so poorly clothed, our dresses and shoes so worn out, that I dared not start for fear your aunt would be ashamed of us. And then, my darling boy, your letter and the twenty-five francs came! I ran quickly to M. Perrin's the merchant, and I bought— pay attention, I am going to tell you all that you have given us, my good and darling boy.

"I bought a good calico dress for Alice, the same for Angéle, a large apron with sleeves for little Marie, three little white bonnets, three good pairs of shoes for their little feet, and I bought for myself a calico dress and a pair of shoes.

"Then I wrote at once to your aunt, that we intended to come. Angéle and I worked so hard, that the dresses and apron were done in four days, so that we were able to wear them while travelling.

"Be happy, my son, in thinking of all the good you have done us.

"But you, my dear boy, how are you clothed? You must want new clothes very much! Dear Jean Paul, do not send us any more money; you see we are almost rich—Louisa is provided for, and Angéle and I have work. The prices for work are very good now at Bagnères; I hope to take back with me to Escaladios enough to live on all the winter. Keep for yourself all that you make. Give it to the mamma that the good God has sent you in Paris, and use it as she tells you to do. Your little sisters send you many kisses. They would like also to send a kiss to my lady and Rosette. Good-bye, my beloved child, I love you so much, and I pray that the good God may protect you.

"P.S. How well you write, Jean Paul! Thanks to your little teacher Madeleine: tell her, my child, as well as her father and mother, that we name them every day in our evening prayer, and ask God to be as good to them as they have been to you. Love them well! love them well!"

"Love them!" said Jean Paul, his eyes full of tears. "As for love, that is not wanting."

While Madeleine was reading it, M. Bienfait had come in, and had seated himself silently.

"Why, this is famous!" said he suddenly, apparently roused from a profound meditation. "So, Jean Paul, your mother does not stand in need of what you earn! What do you think? It is a week since our apprentice left the workshop; and a week ago I said to myself that Jean Paul might take his place. It is a good house, and I shall be there to teach him our

trade.   In three years he would be a good workman,
and earn good wages.   He is large and strong.   Now
tell me, Jean Paul," added he, turning towards our
friend, "will you be a locksmith?   Would you like
that trade, tell me?"

"Formerly—" said our friend, who blushed up to
his ears, and hesitated——

"Say what you think, do not be afraid," answered
M. Bienfait, laughing.

"Formerly—I did not like that trade at all—because
it makes one always so black—and the great heat!"

"And now?" asked M. Bienfait.

"Oh! now," said Jean Paul, who smiled and looked
at his friend, "since I have known you, Monsieur Bienfait, I would like to be the same as you are."

"You are a nice boy," said M. Bienfait, laughing,
and drawing the child to him.

"I just said to myself," continued he, turning to his
wife, "that Jean Paul might continue to exhibit his
mice after dinner.   In the summer he could go to the
public walks, and the cafés, in the winter he could show
them in the streets; after awhile he would be known
in the best parts of the town, and they would make him
go into their houses to amuse the children, as they do
with the man who has the magic lantern.   He could
carry a little bell to let people know when he was passing; I believe in this way he could earn plenty of
money, and at the same time pass his days usefully in
the workshop."

"Well, my friend," said Mme. Bienfait, after a moment's silence, "you might ask your employer at the
same time, if Jean Paul could not have every Thursday

"I HAVE FORGOTTEN MY BEANS!"

229

afternoon. He must go next winter with Madeleine to learn his Catechism, that he may be prepared for his first Communion. Madeleine's mistress has made this agreement."

"Oh! Madeleine's mistress!" interrupted M. Bienfait, smiling. "Madeleine should not have any other mistress than her dear little mamma, who sews like a fairy."

"Yes, but who for ten years that she has lived in her room, knows nothing of the fashions," interrupted Mme. Bienfait in her turn. "Well, you will ask, won't you, if Jean Paul may be free on Thursday?"

"Our master will grant that, he is a good man. Now, Jean Paul," added he, "let it be understood that every evening when the weather will not permit you to go out with your mice, you will read and write at home, and that every Sunday I will give you a lesson, as I do to Madeleine. This will be, I hope, a well regulated life! you will have time neither to idle nor to be dull."

A frightful smell of burning, and a thick smoke, filled the room.

"I am really crazy! I have forgotten my beans! They won't be fit to eat," cried Mme. Bienfait, running to the chimney place and taking the saucepan quickly from the fire.

"Bah! my wife, we are all to blame," said M. Bienfait; "while speaking of Jean Paul, we have forgotten the dinner."

"I will put a little water in them, and a piece of butter, and I hope they may be eatable," said Mme. Bienfait. "I am very sorry; it is unpardonable at my age to be so giddy."

"It was not giddiness, it was because you are too good," said Jean Paul.

They sat down to dinner. The soup was like glue, and so thick that the spoon stood up in the plate.

M. Bienfait made little signs to Madeleine when Mme. Bienfait's back was turned, and the father and daughter laughed very quietly.

The meat was all dried up. M. Bienfait pretended not to be able to eat it. Poor Mme. Bienfait sighed, and asked their pardon. Madeleine laughed in her sleeve and winked at her father; as for Jean Paul, he ate and made no remark. He seemed buried in deep thought.

At last the famous beans came. It was then twilight. Mme. Bienfait gave some of them to each.

"Oh! this, this is too much," cried M. Bienfait. "Wife, I cannot stand this, they are like coal!"

Madeleine now burst out laughing.

"No, no," said Mme. Bienfait, scolding a little, "it is only an idea that you two have; they are a little burnt, but they are still very good. I am sure of it. Let me see!" She put her fork to her lips. "Why, they are disgusting!" cried she. "What a horrid taste!"

"Wife," said M. Bienfait, "I want a light, that we may be able to see these delicious vegetables. I think that you have made a mistake, and that you have fricasseed flannel." Madeleine got up and brought a lighted candle. "Here! look, wife, they are black as ink; you wanted to poison us."

Madeleine brought her plate to the light.

"Mine are blacker than yours and mamma's; but you see they have still the shape of beans; therefore it is very certain that mamma has not put coal in the sauce-pan." She laughed. "Jean Paul, give me your plate, that I may see yours."

"Thank you, Madeleine," said Jean Paul absently.

"Thank me for what?" cried Madeleine in surprise.

Jean Paul answered still absently. "Thank you, I have enough; they are very good. I am no longer hungry."

"Very good! what?"

"The—the things—the beans."

Madeleine looked in Jean Paul's plate. "Papa! mamma! he has eaten them all." She roared out laughing. "Well then, Jean Paul, you found the beans good?" she shook him by the arm.

"Yes, everything is good at Mamma Bienfait's."

"You did not notice that they were horribly burnt?"

"I do not know."

Madeleine said, laughing more and more, "You did not notice that they were all black?"

"I do not know—but I thought there were some beans as black as those."

"And he has eaten them all! all, or a great part of them! Well, mamma, you can say that Jean Paul has great confidence in you."

But Jean Paul said, seriously, "Mamma Bienfait, if I show my mice every day, and all the night, I shall make a great deal of money, and I will make you rich."

Madeleine was still laughing. "Let us see, Jean Paul—is it all the days or all the nights that you want to show them? We want to know that?"

But good Mme. Bienfait would not let this continue. "We understand very well what he says; do not tease him, Madeleine.   My good Jean Paul, all the money that you make will be kept for yourself, I promise you. I will not have one sou more than the six sous daily for your food."

Jean Paul cried.   "But how then shall I be able to make you some return for your kindness to me?   Oh! I see now! it is not with money that I can thank you. I must be so pleasant, so nice, and so good."

M. Bienfait held out his hand to him.   "Remain as you are, my child!"

"But when we have beans like those we had this evening, do not feel obliged to eat them," said Madeleine.

"I hope you will never see any like them again," said Mme. Bienfait.   "It may pass for once."

"And once is too often," said M. Bienfait, looking roguishly at his wife.

CHAPTER XXX

Monsieur Fumeron has his staircase washed by proxy

WINTER had come, and with the winter rain, cold, and short days.

It seemed to our friend Jean Paul that the summer was scarcely over, he had been so much occupied. M. Bienfait's employer had been engaged to do all the locksmith's work of a magnificent new house, and it was M. Bienfait who put the hinges, the gilded locks, upon the doors, the hooks for the curtains, and so on. Jean Paul always went with him. In the street, he carried the leather bag filled with tools; no one would have recognized in this little boy, so clean, so carefully clothed, and who walked so rapidly, the poor little Jean Paul who arrived at Paris the year before, without occupation, half starved, and in rags. While M. Bienfait worked, Jean Paul held his tools for him, or ran back to the shop to bring those he had forgotten. He had looked so much at his friend while he was working that he thought he would be able himself to put the gilded locks upon the doors, and he was crazy to try.

"That will come bye and bye," M. Bienfait told him.

And indeed Jean Paul was permitted to put a lock on the door of the entry.

"Very well done!" said M. Bienfait, who saw him do it.

Thursday at one o'clock, Jean Paul came in as usual to wash and change his blouse, before going to his Catechism. His heart was very light, when he came down the long staircase; he knew his Catechism very well; he had even learnt the portion of the Testament that was to be read next Sunday.

"I shall be there too soon," said he to himself, when he heard the clock strike, "but no, never too soon." He smiled. "I will go over my lesson again in the church, and then as soon as the chapel is opened I will go in. I shall be the first. I feel so happy in that dear chapel. Last Thursday when the clergyman repeated to us those words of the dear Jesus, 'Love your enemies,' I could have almost wished to have had a very wicked enemy, an enemy who had done me a great deal of harm, that I might pardon him immediately, and with all my heart. But I have no enemy, at the workshop all are so good to me!"

Jean Paul, while thinking over these things, had reached the foot of the staircase, and was going through the yard—at least his body, for his mind was with the Catechism. So he did not see M. Fumeron, who was standing at the open window of his lodge, and was making motions to him with his hands and arms. M. Fumeron had a broom in one hand, and in the other a dustbrush of feathers, and was moving them about as a telegraph to attract Jean Paul's attention.

It was useless; Jean Paul's thoughts were with the Catechism, he saw nothing.

M. Fumeron leaned out of the window and said in a very low voice, "My dear little friend."

Jean Paul did not hear him; and went on his way.

"My dear little friend, my dear Jean Paul!" M. Fumeron repeated in a low voice, but doing all he could at the same time to make him hear.

Jean Paul raised his head.

"Come here! come quickly! I have something to say to you, my dear friend."

Jean Paul came near the door of the lodge.

"Don't go that way! not that way!" cried M. Fumeron, still in a low voice. "Come, speak to me here at the window."

Jean Paul obeyed, quite surprised, at being called "My dear friend" by M. Fumeron.

"You see that it would not do to disturb that large gentleman who is speaking to my wife there, before the door of the lodge, my little Jean Paul; he is the owner of this house. He always lives in the country, and in that he is very wise. I do not know what has made him come to Paris to-day, when it is so pleasant in the country. In a word, I must tell you, my dear Jean Paul, that he has come to see his house, and you know my wife does not like me to fatigue myself. For six months I have wanted to clean that horrid back staircase, you understand!"

"Ah! I think you would have done well to have cleaned it, Monsieur Fumeron! for mud, dust, spiders, and many worse things are on it! If I were the owner——"

"You are quite right, my dear little friend," interrupted M. Fumeron, lifting his duster and broom in an agitated manner towards the sky. "Well, look! here is a duster, a broom, a sponge, and a bucket of fresh water; go, my dear Jean Paul, go quickly, and clean up those frightful steps; while I'll go to the owner to keep him from being impatient."

Jean Paul was so astonished at this proposal, that he started back and let all the things fall on the pavement that M. Fumeron had given him.

"My little Jean Paul," he began again in a beseeching voice, and with clasped hands. "You want me to lose my place! you want me to die of hunger!"

"No," answered the child, "but this is Thursday, the day we go to Catechism; I have on my best clothes. It is already late—I must go."

And his inward thought was: "You have always been so cross to me, that I do not feel inclined to do your dirty work."

"But you have plenty of time before the Catechism," M. Fumeron answered in a low voice. "You have still a good half-hour, my little Jean Paul. I beg you to do it!"

Jean Paul did not answer. He saw M. Fumeron no longer, nor his grinning face, still uglier, with its deceitful smile and with its artful expressions of friendship, than it was with its usual brutal expression. No, he heard at the bottom of his heart, the voice of Jesus, which repeated, "Love your enemies." "Do good to those who hate you." He remained a moment motionless; then without saying a word to M. Fumeron, he stooped down, picked up the broom, the duster, and the sponge, took the bucket and went towards the staircase. He ran up into his room, took off his new blouse, turned up the sleeves of his shirt, as well as the legs of his trowsers, and began resolutely his disagreeable

task.   All at once he stopped; he just then remembered
that there were one hundred and ten steps to this terrible
staircase.   He heaved a deep sigh, and began his work
again with more ardor than ever.

The higher stories were cleaned very easily, and very
fast.   But those below were incrusted with dirt, owing
principally to that horrid dyer, and his nasty drugs.   At
last Jean Paul had washed them all; he was as red as
fire.   He put the brush and other utensils in a dark
corner of the vestibule, and went and washed himself
at the pump in the yard.   He saw the owner, who, con-
ducted by M. Fumeron, crossed the yard, and went
towards the staircase.

"I did not finish them too soon," said our friend to
himself.

He ran up as fast as he could to his little room, put
on his blouse, took his books and went down stairs
again.   Just as he passed before the lodge, he was
seized by the strong arm of Mme. Fumeron, who held
him forcibly, in spite of all his efforts to get away.
The owner was still there, he was just going to leave.
He was delighted with the way his house was kept, and
he showed his satisfaction by giving a five-franc piece
to Mme. Fumeron.

As soon as the proprietor's back was turned, Mme.
Fumeron put the five-franc piece in Jean Paul's hand.

"You have earned it fairly, my poor child, I saw all
that was going on from the corner of my eye; you have
done us a great service," she said.

But a hand was slipped in Jean Paul's hand before
he could shut it, and had taken away the piece.

"How can you do that, my wife?" said M. Fumeron.

putting the piece in his waistcoat pocket, and buttoning his great coat over it, to make it more sure. "If any one has earned the piece it is I; for was it not my idea to make Jean Paul clean the staircase?"

Mme. Fumeron ran after her husband, who went into the lodge.

"Stay there, my boy," she said to Jean Paul; "you shall have the piece in five minutes."

But Jean Paul, instead of waiting, took to his heels, and ran as fast as he could. "I did that for the sake of God," he said, "I do not want to be paid for it. I would not have done it for five francs. And then, my poor Catechism! How late I am! There is half past two striking by the church clock! I will arrive at least a half an hour too late! Oh how vexed I am!"

Chapter XXXI

Jean Paul is misunderstood

A LITTLE after four o'clock, all the children came out from the Catechism. For a few minutes the church steps were filled with a crowd of little girls and boys, who soon went off into the neighboring streets.

Madeleine and Jean Paul joined each other as usual, and returned together to the old house. Thursday, after Catechism, they had holiday, and often took advantage of it to take a nice walk together. But this day, although it was fine weather, they seemed sad, and walked silently along.

"Madeleine," Jean Paul said suddenly, "promise me to do what I am going to ask you."

"First ask me, and I will promise afterwards."

"No, you must promise first," said Jean Paul.

"Tell me what you want to ask me," she answered.

"No, I have thought of it too long for that; if you were to refuse me, it would trouble me very much. First promise!"

"There is no harm at least, in what you want to make me do?"

"Madeleine! how could you think so?"

"Oh, I promise," Madeleine said quickly.

"Honor bright?"

"Honor bright! Tell me quick, what have I promised?"

241

"You have promised to come with me to buy a dress for one of my sisters. Come, let us run to the boulevard Sebastopol. There are some fine shops there, and here is the money." He drew from his pocket a little bundle of paper. "There are six francs."

Madeleine seemed angry as well as surprised: "I thought you gave all your money to mamma."

Jean Paul was embarrassed. "I gave her all the big pieces—but I saved this. I can assure you that I made this besides. And then I knew that my sister was absolutely in need of a dress."

"Your sister! which sister? Your mother wrote that they all had new dresses. Is it for Angéle?"

"No, and I will not tell you for which one."

"For Caroline?"

"No."

"For little Marie?"

"No."

"Then it is for—Oh! what's her name? I have forgotten her name. What is it then?"

"Bravo! forget her name as much as you will! but come with me at once and choose the dress while there is still a little light. You know the stuffs ladies wear, while I, you know, could not tell wadding from Satan."

"Satin, not Satan." Madeleine smiled, but began again more seriously, and even made a little face: "But I assure you I do not feel inclined to laugh, Jean Paul; mamma will be very much displeased. I know that she is saving all your money, to buy six new shirts for you. No, come, let us go back home, be good. I'll let you go all alone. I am going to leave you."

"And it is this that Madeleine calls, 'Honor bright!'

Well, good-bye, Madeleine, I will buy my dress by myself; I will make a very poor purchase, but I will spend my six francs all the same." The two children separated, the one going one way, and one the other.

Soon Madeleine came back to Jean Paul, sighing deeply: "I have promised! I must go with you. Besides, since you will buy this dress, it is better that it should be well chosen. Then it is for— What's her name? for——"

Jean Paul laughed: "You have hit it!—it is for——"

They had arrived before one of those immense shops, large as a town, and were stopping to admire the goods in the window. The daylight was over, all the lamps were lighted, which seemed to redouble the splendor of the silks.

"Tell me, Madeline, you would like very much, wouldn't you, that fine red Satan dress with white spots?" He pointed out to her a showy evening dress.

"I," cried Madeleine, "ah! ah! what should I do with your Satan when it rained on Sundays, or even when it did not rain?"

"You name it well—Satan, my pretty child," said a mild, grave, and tremulous voice behind her. "These handsome dresses have often tempted and hurried into evil more than one young girl."

Jean Paul and Madeleine, quite ashamed that any one had overheard their conversation, hurried into the shop.

Madeleine chose a stuff of blue and black, which she said would be still prettier in daytime, and would last very long.

It was measured, and cut, and was wrapped up in gray paper, and the neat bundle was handed to Jean Paul.

Jean Paul paid for it, went out of the shop, took Madeleine by the hand, and ran along with her to the old house.

Jean Paul put his bundle in his room, and joined Madeleine again at her mother's.

It was late. Both hurried to set the table. They had hardly finished, when M. Bienfait came in, and they sat down to dinner.

"Well, children," said M. Bienfait, after they had eaten their soup, and their hunger was a little satisfied, "well, children, is not this Thursday? And you have not yet spoken of the Catechism! Come, then, give us some account of it."

"Very bad, father, very bad," said Madeleine quickly.

"What, very bad?" M. Bienfait turned towards Jean Paul. "Very bad, Jean Paul?"

Jean Paul bent his head over his plate, blushed, and did not answer.

Madeleine said in a very lively manner, "I will tell you all about it, father. There are always some children who come very late, and every Thursday Monsieur Bordiac, the director of the Catechism, scolds them, and advises them to come earlier the next time. To-day there were more children late than usual, and the one who arrived last, the last of all, was Jean Paul. The prayer was said, the psalm was sung, and they had almost finished saying the Catechism; and then——"

M. Bienfait turned to Jean Paul. "How did that

happen, my child? you left the workshop at half-past twelve o'clock, didn't you?"

Jean Paul nodded yes.

Madeleine began again, talking hurriedly: "Well, I did not quit the workshop until one o'clock, and my workshop is a great deal further from the church than Jean Paul's—and I arrived before the prayer was begun."

Now Mme. Bienfait spoke severely: "What were you doing, Jean Paul, all that time? Where were you? Answer."

Jean Paul held his head still lower down over his plate, and blushed more than ever.

Madeleine talked with great animation. "And then, father, Monsieur Bordiac was very much dissatisfied, and he said that——"

M. Bienfait interrupted her: "Hush, Madeleine! you stun us with your noise. Come, Jean Paul, answer. Where were you? and what were you doing in that time?"

"Why don't you answer, Jean Paul?" asked Madeleine. "You left a half an hour before me, and I arrived in good time."

Jean Paul said in a very low voice, with tears in his eyes, "Naughty Madeleine!"

Madeleine became more and more animated. "And why don't you answer when my father speaks to you? Father, who is so good to you! See, mamma, Jean Paul has all sorts of mysteries to-day. After Catechism, he went and bought a dress for his sister, with the money which he had put away, and hid."

Jean Paul got up, his face wet with tears. "Naughty, naughty Madeleine!"

He opened the door, and shut it to violently, then ran and hid himself in his room.

In Mme. Bienfait's room they continued to eat silently.

"Madeleine talks too much, and she loves to govern others too much!" the good Mme. Bienfait said, slowly and mildly.

It was Madeleine's turn to hold down her head. The dinner was finished very sadly, without another word being spoken.

After dinner M. Bienfait took a book; and Mme. Bienfait and Madeleine cleared away the table.

Meanwhile the chamber door was opened very softly, and they saw looking in a pleasant round face all smiling, though still wet with tears. It was Jean Paul. He ran to Madeleine, and threw his arms around her.

"Madelichon," he said to her, "I can't be angry with you. I can't indeed! or if I want to be so, I must go to some other place than my room. Just now, when I went there, it seemed to me that I became the Jean Paul of old times; abandoned, miserable, without a friend! Who has made me happy, who has taken care of me, who has loved me? You all; and you, Madeleine, first of all. Yes, I am very sure that I was in the wrong, that I am always wrong; and that you are always right. So, I am going to tell you; this dress—but where is it then? I know I brought it with me."

"You have let it fall," said Mme. Bienfait picking up a bundle from the floor, "and you are walking over it. Fortunately it is wrapped up."

"Well, I did not dare to tell you for which of my sisters it was intended."

"Louise! I have found her name," said Madeleine.

"Not at all." Jean Paul kissed her. "It is for my sister here." He pointed to Madeleine. "It has been a long time since I heard Mamma Bienfait say that you wanted a dress. Do you think it is pretty? I wanted to keep it for Sunday, your birthday, but Mademoiselle Madelichon does not like mysteries."

Madeleine was quite touched. "You are too good, Jean Paul. I ought to have guessed that this dress was for me. But you kept saying, 'It is for my sister.' "

"Well, have I not told the truth? Have you not all been to me a father, a mother, a good little sister, Madeleine?"

He went around the room and embraced them all, as he always did when his gratitude overflowed. Mme. Bienfait gave him a little tap on his cheek: "I have a great mind to scold you," said she, "you have spent your money foolishly."

Madeleine leaned towards Jean Paul.

"I did not deserve this pretty dress," said she to him. "I have given you pain, pardon me."

Jean Paul put his hand on her mouth.

"And then," he said aloud, and jumping with joy, "the idea that tormented me the most when I was in my room, was that Madeleine would have all the dishes to wash, which would soil her hands. Quick! how late I am!"

"Good, good Jean Paul!" said Madeleine, with tears in her eyes.

At last the dinner-table is cleared, the dishes are

washed, and everything is put in order in Mme. Bienfait's room. But it is too late for Madeleine or Jean Paul to begin to sew or to read. They finished the evening talking together near the window. Madeleine was seated on a chair, Jean Paul on a stool at her feet; it was his favorite place.

Madeleine did not remember the gentle reproach that her mother had made her, for she still talked a great deal, and with more animation than ever. Jean Paul scarcely answered, and spoke so low that Madeleine had to lean towards him to hear him.

Suddenly she got up and came to her mother.

"Mamma," said she, "I am too wicked; I am positively detestable."

M. and Mme. Bienfait stopped their reading and work, and fixed their eyes upon her; they felt inclined to laugh at this sudden confession.

"Mother and father," she said, "do you know why this poor Jean Paul that I worried so much to-day at dinner came too late to the Cat ——"

Jean Paul jumped up, ran to her, and put his hand on her mouth.

"Do not tell it, Madeleine! do not tell it, I beg of you."

"Oh! but I did not promise this time: On the contrary, I will tell all. Well, mamma, he came too late to the Catechism because he washed our staircase from top to bottom."

"What, our staircase? and why did he do it?" cried M. Bienfait.

"That is the reason that it is so clean!" cried Mme. Bienfait. "I was enchanted this afternoon, coming up, and I said to myself, M. Fumeron is turning over a new leaf."

"Not at all, mamma! it was this poor Jean Paul who washed them from one end to the other, before going to Catechism."

M. Bienfait said roguishly, "The time was badly chosen——"

"No, no, my little father, the owner was there, and Monsieur Fumeron said to Jean Paul that if he did not wash the staircase quickly for them the owner would turn them out. This old Fumeron begged Jean Paul so much——" she stopped and turned quickly towards Jean Paul. "I believe that this Fumeron was always very cross to you?"

Jean Paul said, "That was the very reason I did not want to refuse him."

Madeleine went up to Mme. Bienfait. "Oh! mother, see! Monsieur Fumeron was cross to him—he did his work—Madeline teased him—he bought her a dress. I really feel like crying. I am as bad as Monsieur Fumeron."

She was silent, and held down her head.

Mme. Bienfait looked at her thoughtfully, although half laughing.

Madeleine took her handkerchief from her pocket to wipe her eyes, and began to cry very much; a little match box fell upon the floor.

"Oh! how thoughtless I am!" said she, laughing through her tears. "It is only now that I have thought of this!"

She picked up the little box, and threw it to Jean Paul.

"Look! that will console me a little. You will see that I am not always so bad as I have been this evening. Every day lately, at the workshop, I have worked for you at lunch hours. Come, look at all this by the lamp; that will amuse you. Do you see?" she said opening the little box, and taking from it all sorts of little things. "My lady was not in the latest fashion. I must tell you, Jean Paul, that crinolines are not worn now. Look at this little narrow skirt of violet-colored silk, with a long train. It is disgraceful, isn't it? and this large bow of violet-colored ribbon to fasten up the train when it is muddy; what do you say to that? Then here is a trimmed petticoat to wear under the dress, and a pork-pie hat."

Madeleine stopped—she seemed quite vexed.

"Oh! what a misfortune!" she said.

"What is it?" said Jean Paul, quite uneasy.

"My hat does not fit," said Madeleine. "I had forgotten that my lady had no chignon. It would be impossible to wear one of these hats without a chignon. This is distressing!"

"Make her one, then," said Mme. Bienfait, laughing.

"Still more impossible!" said Madeleine. "She has not hair enough."

"If it were only the ladies who had much hair, who wore chignons," answered Mme. Bienfait, "we would see very few of them. Here, take this little piece of white wadding, roll it, and fasten it to the hat."

"Hurrah! hurrah!" said Jean Paul. "Oh! the beautiful hair of my lady! I will bring them to try on all these beautiful things. It is wonderful! Madelinette, how nice you are!"

A moment after Jean Paul came back, bringing his little animals with him.

"Let us try on all the new clothes at once. Look, here is the dress; put it on her——"

"How droll this dress is!" said Jean Paul, who was turning it every way. "I thought it was a violet-colored silk, and it is black, and made of wool."

"You have left your eyes in your room, my poor Jean Paul. What! do you not see that it is a cloth riding habit, and made of fine black cloth! all the fashionable ride on horseback now, and I wanted to make a riding habit for Rosette."

"For my lady, you mean."

Madeleine tried hard to restrain a laugh. "For Rosette."

Jean Paul looked at the table. "And the hat with the chignon——"

"A hat with a chignon worn with a riding habit! Who ever heard of such a thing? Jean Paul, what taste you have! Look! there is a real man's hat with a green veil, and a riding whip! It was a match which I covered with kid. Now, Jean Paul, dress Rosette; you seem quite confounded."

Jean Paul began to dance the mountain dance in the middle of the room.

"Not so astonished as you think, Mademoiselle Madeleine! I beg you to show me now the handsome violet-colored silk dress, and the hat and chignon, which you hid while I was in my room. You are playing a farce with me; you have made two complete costumes, one for my lady and one for Rosette." He danced around the room. "And I am so happy! so happy!"

At last Jean Paul became more calm, and sat down by Madeleine quite out of breath. They both dressed my lady and her maid in their new costumes, which were pronounced delicious, lovely, and not to be surpassed; and our heroines were as much admired as if they were making their first appearance.

Chapter XXXII

Jean Paul regains his reputation

A WEEK has passed. It is Thursday. Our big and little friends have just sat down to dinner.

"Well, father," Madeleine began before she was scarcely seated. "You do not ask us how our Catechism passed to-day. It is Thursday however. Oh! if you knew!"

"My child, take time to eat your soup, I beg of you."

Madeleine ate two spoonfuls and then began again. "Oh! if you only knew, father! to-day we both arrived early. They had hardly said the prayers and recited the lessons, when Monsieur Bordiac cried out in a loud voice, 'Jean Paul!' and then Jean Paul got up, as red as fire."

"But how did you see that?" demanded Mme. Bienfait. "I thought you sat on the fourth bench behind Jean Paul."

"But I saw the back of his neck, which was quite red, I assure you. And now let me tell you what Monsieur Bordiac said: 'Jean Paul, is it a great sin to come too late to Catechism?'

"Jean Paul did not answer aloud, but I saw by the motion of his head, that he said yes.

" 'I do not say that for you,' said Monsieur Bordiac, 'for generally you are in very good time; but I want to

253

ask you if it is a very great fault to arrive once by chance too late at the Catechism?'

" 'Yes, Monsieur,' answered Jean Paul, with his good strong voice.

" 'Even if one stays at home to do a good action,' said Monsieur Bordiac.

" 'Yes, Monsieur,' said Jean Paul.

"Then Monsieur Bordiac began to laugh, and all the children too."

Jean Paul interrupted Madeleine. "I did not know very well what he asked me; I was so frightened; I only knew that I had come too late last Thursday."

Madeleine continued. "Monsieur Bordiac went on as if he wanted to teach Jean Paul a little.

" 'But now, my child, if, for example, you remained at home to do a great service to a friend, or even an enemy, would you be very guilty for coming a little too late to your Catechism?'

" 'Yes,' Jean Paul still answered.

"Everybody laughed—Monsieur Bordiac, the mammas, and the children.

" 'Well, my dear friend,' said Monsieur Bordiac, 'you are too severe.' "

"You forget, Madeleine," said Jean Paul, "that he added immediately, 'However, my children, you must remember that in general, the best act you can do is to arrive punctually at the hour of the Catechism.' "

Madeleine interrupted him: "And then he said, 'Come, get a picture, Jean Paul.' "

Jean Paul continued: "When I came quite near him, he gave me a pretty picture, and said to me in a low voice, 'I have scratched out the bad mark I gave you last Thursday for want of punctuality. Continue, my child, to love those who hate you, and God will bless you."

"So you see, father, how strange it is! The persons who teach the Catechism know all that the children do."

Then it was M. Bienfait's turn to laugh. "Particularly when the mammas of these children go and pay them visits."

And Mme. Bienfait laughed also. "But, my friend, I would not let Monsieur Bordiac think that my Jean Paul was an idler and wasted his time."

Madeleine was quite astonished. "Why, mamma! have you been to see Monsieur Bordiac? you have dared to go to his house!"

"Certainly; many mothers visit the clergymen. It is the least they can do to thank them for all the trouble they take in instructing their naughty children. Monsieur Bordiac is very well satisfied with Jean Paul and Madeleine, I am glad to say; and he hopes they will be prepared to make their first Communion this year."

When spring came, Jean Paul and Madeleine went to the church on the holy day which was to make them its members. As they knelt before the altar, side by side, each said a little prayer for the other, before their thoughts turned wholly to God. When the day was over, they took off their special garments, and went back to their humble work. But their hearts kept on joyously singing the praises of the dear, good, merciful God.

CHAPTER XXXIII

A mystery

TWO years had passed. Jean Paul had become a skilful workman. His apprenticeship was nearly over.

Madeleine stayed at home, and worked with her mother. They were never either one of them without plenty of work; but it was health which failed them. Every winter M. Bienfait had some attacks of his painful rheumatism, and Mme. Bienfait was often confined to her chamber for months with a cold.

This winter seemed to be harder for our friends than usual. It was not a cold this time, but it was that terrible bronchitis that had again attacked Mme. Bienfait; for a month she was confined to her bed, and scarcely left it.

There was another bed made in the little room for M. Bienfait, who was kept there by his frightful rheumatism. For Madeleine could not bear the idea of his returning to the hospital. She took care of them both, and she and Jean Paul took turns in sitting up with them at night.

At last they are better, those dearly loved parents. They have left their beds, and are sitting near the fireplace. But their convalescence lasted all winter. When Jean Paul came back from his work, he was struck with the thinness of Madeleine, and her pallid looks.

Although she had great need of rest, the poor little thing worked early and late. She was afraid of losing her customers; and besides she was the only one in the house who earned anything.

Jean Paul's apprenticeship was not yet finished. It was in vain that he tried to show my lady and Rosette. The poor ladies had become very old. Their backs were bent, their legs trembled, and their long hair fell around their throats like long white beards. They needed rest also—the rest of old age.

Meanwhile, as the spring approached, Madeleine began to hope. She thought that the heat would restore the health of her dear parents. She thought also, that very soon the three years of Jean Paul's apprenticeship would be over. Madeleine had made all her calculations; with what she made, and the little savings her parents had put aside before their sickness, she had just enough money to last until Jean Paul's apprenticeship was over.

"Dear Madeleine," he said to her very often, "when shall I earn good wages, and bring you my money in the evening? You will then have time to rest, won't you? and I shall again see your gay face of old."

Jean Paul had become the life of the house; when he came in, happy and strong, to his dinner, it seemed like a ray of sunshine. He told M. Bienfait all that was done in the workshop; he made Madeleine laugh; he talked for a long time with Mme. Bienfait and caressed her.

One evening, however, he seemed full of care. He talked, and even laughed, but it was with effort.

The next day he did not laugh; and talked very little.

His eyes were fixed upon vacancy, for he did not seem to see anything.

The third day he was quite gloomy and silent. Madeleine could not help asking him why he was so sad. But Jean Paul neither heard nor answered her. After dinner, he felt in his pocket.

"A letter from my mother," he said, "that Madame Fumeron gave to me. I had forgotten that."

He drew near the lamp, and seemed to read it eagerly. He finished the letter, then read it over again, folded it, and put it in his pocket.

"Is your mother well?" asked the good Madeleine.

"Yes, thank you," answered Jean Paul.

"Your sisters? and everybody?" asked Madeleine again, who hoped that Jean Paul would as usual read his mother's letter aloud.

"Everybody is well, thank you," said Jean Paul.

Then he helped Madeleine to clear away the table, and put the dishes in order. He did not talk, and twice he was very near letting a plate fall that he carried. Besides, he did not seem to know what he was about, for he put the soup tureen in the wardrobe, and the remains of the butter in the drawer of the bureau. Madeleine saw it all, and put the things in order without saying a word.

M. and Mme. Bienfait went to bed early. Madeleine sat up, and worked alongside of them.

Jean Paul had gone to his room.

In about an hour, M. Bienfait fell asleep. Madeleine heard some one knock softly at the door. She got up on tiptoe to open it.

It was Jean Paul. He beckoned to her to come out

and speak to him in the entry, so as not to wake up her parents.

Madeleine went out of the room, and shut the door softly.

"Madeleine," said Jean Paul, in so low and trembling a voice, that she could hardly hear him. "Have you still those twenty-five francs that your mother put away before she was sick, to buy me a coat?"

"Certainly," said Madeleine, blushing, "they are in the drawer."

"Then, will you give them to me?"

Madeleine was quite confounded. "Why did not Jean Paul ask for them before my mother?" she said to herself.

"But—" said she, quite embarrassed.

"They are mine," said Jean Paul quickly. "Give them to me."

"Oh! immediately," said Madeleine, wounded at Jean Paul's tone.

She went back into the room and came out again in a minute, holding a little bundle of paper in her hand.

"Here they are," said she, giving them to Jean Paul.

"And now, good-bye, Madeleine," he said, turning his head away, and taking her by the hand; "pray to the good God for me. I am going to start to-morrow for Escaladios."

He stopped suddenly, ran into his room, and shut the door violently.

Madeleine remained a few minutes, motionless, at the place where he had left her. She came to her friend's

door. She wanted to speak to him—it was impossible
that he could go away in this manner. Just as she
was going to knock, she let her hand fall again. It
seemed to her that it was no longer the same Jean
Paul of old. She went into her mother's room, sat
down and began to work again. But she did not do a
single stitch. She remained with her eyes fixed, and
full of tears.

"Meanwhile, he is there yet," she said to herself,
"just near me. If I were to wake up father, and tell
him all! Jean Paul must not go away in this manner."

She got up and came to the bed, and looked for a
moment at her father's thin face.

"No," said she, "sleep on, dear father, forget your
pains, and rest yourself."

It struck eleven o'clock.

"And I am doing nothing, and am letting the lamp
burn! so wasteful as I am!"

She went into her little room, said a long prayer,
and went to bed, but it was not to sleep. She did not
want to sleep, she listened for the least sound.

"I shall hear him get up," said she, "and I will not
let him go away."

However, towards the morning, her tired eyes closed.

It was bright day when she heard her mother come
to her chamber door and say to her father,

"Our Madeleine is still asleep. So much the better;
poor child, she has great need of rest."

Madeleine jumped up, and dressed quickly. She
ran to Jean Paul's door. The key was in the lock.
She knocked once, twice, no answer; she went in, there
was no one there, the room was empty. She ran hastily

down to Mme. Fumeron. The good woman had seen
Jean Paul go out at six o'clock in the morning.

"Did he speak to you?" asked Madeleine.

"No, he seemed in a great hurry. He carried a big
bundle at the end of a stick."

Madeleine did not answer. She flew across the yard
like an arrow, ran up the long staircase, went into her
mother's room, and fell quite breathless into a chair.

She was as white as a sheet. Her mother came to her
and took her hand.

"You should not run up so quickly, darling," said
she to her. "And why do you go so often up and down
that tiresome staircase?"

"Oh! mamma, it is nothing," answered Madeleine,
who was thinking how she could tell her parents of the
departure of Jean Paul without giving them pain.

"Oh! Oh! my darling, you are almost fainting!"
said M. Bienfait. "Give her a little wine, wife. Where
is your pain, dear child?"

"Nowhere, darling father, it is—you see—Jean
Paul——"

"Jean Paul?" repeated Madame Bienfait.

"He has gone away, mamma, he has gone back to
his own country."

"It is impossible!" interrupted M. Bienfait. "He
was here last night as usual, and he did not think of
leaving us."

"When you were asleep, father and mother, he called
me and asked me for his money," continued Madeleine.
"You know, mamma, his twenty-five francs, that were
left from his last summer's money. I did not dare
to refuse him, and then he told me that he was going

away the next morning. I have been to Madame Fumeron's. She saw him going out this morning very
early with a bundle."

"And why did he go off this way, without telling
us?" asked M. Bienfait.

"I do not know," answered Madeleine, "I only know
that he received a letter from his mother yesterday."

"His mother is perhaps very ill," suggested Mme.
Bienfait.

"I do not think so," answered Madeleine. "He told
me that everybody was well, and besides, the letter was
long, and beautifully written; at least it looked so
to me."

"It is very strange," said M. Bienfait, sighing deeply,
"that this child, who loved us so much, should go off
without saying good-bye, or speaking an affectionate
word to us."

Mme. Bienfait did not answer; she would not look
at her husband or Madeleine, for her eyes were filled
with tears.

"What fine weather!" said M. Bienfait. "I will go
out and take a little turn. I am tired of staying in the
house."

This was the first time for three months that M.
Bienfait had crossed the threshold of his door.

"My father! my friend!" cried Mme. Bienfait and
Madeleine at the same time.

"Are you strong enough to walk the street?" added
Mme. Bienfait.

"I will go with you," said Madeleine, running at
once to get her bonnet and shawl.

"I feel very well; it is very mild weather, and I

want to go out alone," said M. Bienfait, emphasizing each word.

He did not add that he wanted to go to the workshop to speak about Jean Paul.

He came in but a short time before dinner. Mme. Bienfait and Madeleine ran to meet him.

"You are tired," cried Madeleine.

"No, no, my child, no," he answered, a little roughly.

He sat down upon a chair, and Madeleine finished setting the table.

"Ah, well," said M. Bienfait, after a moment's silence; "I have just come from the workshop."

"And has he really started for Escaladios?" said Mme. Bienfait.

"I only saw the new apprentice, that young German. He was taking care of the shop. The owner was out."

"What did he tell you father?"

"When I asked him where Jean Paul was, he said that he would not be there to-day, he had gone to his own country, very, very far off; his apprenticeship was over."

"So a child, a stranger, knew that Jean Paul had started! It must have been a settled plan for a long time! He has spoken of it to everybody excepting us," said Madeleine.

"I waited for the return of the master until nightfall, but in vain," said M. Bienfait. "I would perhaps have learned from him something more positive."

"It is true," continued Madeleine thoughtfully," that his apprenticeship is over. He knows his trade; he can now gain his livelihood. He does not need us any longer. He will return to his mother, and forget us just as you most need him."

"Come, come, let us sit down to dinner," said the good Mme. Bienfait, wishing to put a stop to this painful conversation.

All three sat down. There was one place empty.

"And I set a plate for him, fool that I was!" murmured Madeleine.

She got up hurriedly, and took away hastily the glass, the plate, and the spoon which she had placed for Jean Paul. The tears ran down her cheeks.

"The ungrateful fellow, to leave you this way, my darling parents, and after all that you have done for him! I would have liked better never to have known him. I hate the day when I went for the first time to look at his mice, and when I made his acquaintance."

"Child," said M. Bienfait, mildly and seriously, "regret nothing. We have done good to Jean Paul, and we must not repent that we have done it. If he is ungrateful, it is he who is to be pitied. God perhaps brought him to us to give us an opportunity of doing a little good. Is our good action blotted out by the sudden departure of your friend, dear little Madeleine?" he said tenderly to her, at the same time putting his hand under the chin of his daughter, and forcing her to raise her head and look at him.

"You are right, darling father," said she; "but it is very hard."

"Do not let us speak of it any more," said M. Bienfait.

He began to speak of the walks that he had taken that day, and of the shops he had seen, and so on; he

tried to be gay, but when he had done talking, Mme.
Bienfait and Madeleine sighed, and did not answer.

All three thought of Jean Paul. He knew all the
news, he sang all the pretty new songs of the time!
and then when anything was wanting upon the table,
how he jumped from his chair to run and get it, and
gave it laughing to whoever wanted it! Where is he,
this dear Jean Paul? Where is he?

Just as the dinner was finished Madeleine broke the
silence.

"Positively I will not speak any more of him—it
gives me too much pain!" cried she.

"Then why do you speak of him, darling child?"
said Mme. Bienfait, kissing her affectionately.

"I can't help thinking of him!" replied she, with
tears in her eyes, "the room seems quite empty, doesn't
it, father?"

"Not when you are in it, dear Madelinette," answered he, forcing a smiling. But in truth he thought
as she did.

Chapter XXXIV

My lady and Rosette do not go on the journey

TWO days, three days passed. Our friends were weighed down with grief. Madeleine was paler than ever; her father and mother seemed also more unwell. None of them spoke of Jean Paul, but they all thought of him and suffered.

One afternoon, Madeleine was working very hard to finish a dress for one of her customers. She stopped short—put her head forward, and held her ear to listen. Her needle rested in the air, in the hand that held it. She threw the dress on the table, and ran out of the room like lightning. M. and Mme. Bienfait looked quite astonished. Before they had time to say a word to each other, Madeleine had come back.

"Mamma! Papa!" said she, "he has left my lady and Rosette! look! here they are in this cage with this big piece of bread, which must have been much larger when he started! Father, he will come back, you will see! he will be back by the time the bread is eaten! My dear little lady, and you Rosette, you are very sad, aren't you, at the departure of your good master? So you must remain here, and we will keep you company, and take care of you. And I who did not see you when I went into Jean Paul's room the day he left! Excuse me, I was so agitated."

"And you are very much excited to-day, my child, for you have left the door of Jean Paul's room open; I hear it slamming," said Mme. Bienfait.

Madeleine went out again, and then came back triumphant.

"And his book, dear mamma! he has left his father's beautiful book! Oh! now you will not say as you did a little while ago by the motion of your head, that he will not come back! won't he return, father?"

"I do not know, my child. In his hurried departure he may have forgotten his mice, and his precious book," said M. Bienfait.

"Oh, no! darling father; you will see, you will see!"

That day, and the next, Madeleine was very gay. Her father and mother were so happy in seeing her so, that they became almost as gay as she. M. Bienfait spoke of going to his work again. He had only a pain in one of his arms, he said.

"Stay at home, darling father," answered Madeleine, singing; "and, my lady and Rosette, do you eat as fast as possible the food that Jean Paul has left you, so that he may come home sooner."

Chapter XXXV

M. and Mme. Fumeron lose two lodgers

THE next morning the bread was eaten—Madeleine had given them more—and Jean Paul had not appeared.

As she did every day, Madeleine went out to buy provisions. When she came home, she found at Mme. Fumeron's a letter addressed to her. The handwriting was very familiar, and the post-mark was Escaladios.

Madeleine had been so sure that her friend would return that day, that she attached very little importance to the poor letter. She entered very quietly into the room, unpacked her basket of provisions, and at last held out her hand to her father.

"A letter from Jean Paul," said she, carelessly.

"What does he say?" said Mme. Bienfait quickly.

"It will be very easy to know, for it is very well written. Jean Paul does honor to his teacher," said M. Bienfait, while breaking the seal; then he read aloud:

"My Madeleine, mamma Bienfait, and father:
I must relate all to you—but—no, first of all I must embrace all three of you.

"My Madeleine, the house is rented; M. Legras, the owner, wished me to take it. But you cannot understand. I must explain it to you.

"Do you know, Madeleine, I was very much worried at Paris. For some time past our emplover had very

268

little work, and just when I expected to make money for you, and my parents, he told me that he was going to sell his shop, and that I would have to look for work elsewhere. I looked for it—but I could not find any! Then I remembered that my mother had written a good while ago, that the old blacksmith was dead, that he had amassed quite a nice sum of money for his children, and that there was no one at the forge now, which was a great pity. I thought of it over and over again, and then my mother wrote me word that M. Legras had not been able to rent his forge since the death of the old blacksmith, and that he was quite vexed about it.

"It was forever in my thoughts. And then I saw placarded on all the walls of Paris, in letters as big as my head, 'Excursion trains to Toulouse, return tickets, twenty-five francs.' (This is the advantage of knowing how to read. Thanks to you, Madeleine.)

"Then you must know, Madeleine, that all this seethed in my head as the famous black beans did in mamma Bienfait's saucepan. I said, 'If M. Bienfait rents the forge, we could work there together, and he could make money as the old smith did. Madeleine and mamma Bienfait could work with my mother. The summer will soon be here; then they will all go to Bigorre, and the waters of Bigorre will cure mamma Bienfait's cough, and my father's rheumatism.' Madeleine, these waters are so good that they cure even the Parisian ladies and gentlemen who have nothing the matter with them.

"Then, Madelinette, I started off as if mad. My mother was quite surprised at seeing me. She hardly recognized me, I had grown so much, and you had taken such care of me! and I should not have recognized my little sisters. But we will speak of them bye-and-bye.

"Then, Madeleine, after having asked the advice of my mother, I went to look for M. Legras. He has promised to rent the forge to your father, if your father wants it. You cannot imagine how pretty the house at the forge is—a large parlor, and two pretty rooms, without counting the workshop—and there is a very pretty garden! We shall be able to keep a cow and chickens. But I will not tell you any more to-day; I must keep something to talk about, Madeleine. I will be with you almost as soon as my letter. I am coming for you.

"My respects to my parents.

"JEAN PAUL.

"Will you look in my room to see if my lady and Rosette have still enough to eat?

"Mother is writing to your mother; she will explain it all much better than I can do. I forgot to tell you that the forge and the little garden rent for a hundred francs a year."

A letter from Jean Paul's mother came the next day, and confirmed all that Jean Paul had written; she said that the old smith had done very well for a great many years, and that the house was pretty.

"My good little Jean Paul!" cried Madeleine. "It was I who was ungrateful! We will go to Escaladios, won't we, father?" she said warmly, looking at her father.

"What do you think of it?" asked M. Bienfait of his wife.

"And you?" she said in her turn.

"This plan pleases me very well," answered M. Bienfait. "It is worth thinking of—living has become so dear in Paris!"

"Particularly when one is sick in the winter," said Madeleine. "If those waters could cure you, my dear parents?"

"They have cured a great many persons," said M. Bienfait. "And then only one hundred francs a year for a pretty house and garden, when we pay here almost double for this small chamber, and Madeleine's closet!"

"Well, well, it is settled. Let us start! let us start!" cried Madeleine, clapping her hands.

"And the money for the journey?" said Mme. Bienfait.

"We shall be able to get that by selling our furniture," said M. Bienfait.

Mme. Bienfait looked with regret on her bed, and on her pretty bureau, that she had taken care of so lovingly since her marriage.

"What can you do?" said her husband, who understood her look. "They are old friends, it is true; but we cannot carry them with us. If you should recover your health, and Madeleine become robust, I should regret nothing."

"Nor I either, dear friend; when you have recovered your health and strength I shall be quite happy."

The next day but one after, Jean Paul arrived like a thunder clap. He nearly broke open the door, in order to get in more quickly, that he might smother his friends with kisses. He wanted them to start the same evening.

"Wait a minute," said M. Bienfait, "it will be necessary for me to raise some money before starting."

"Let us start! let us start!" repeated Jean Paul.

His friends had a great deal of trouble to make him understand that they could only carry their clothes to Escaladios, and that they must sell all the rest. Jean Paul appeared distressed. "It will take so long!" said he. He consoled himself by getting Madeleine to buy, with some money his mother had given him, a large trunk, which he made them bring and place in the middle of his friends' room, and in which he heaped pell-mell all that he could put his hands upon.

"That is so much done!" said he.

"And so much to be undone!" thought Mme. Bienfait, who made up her mind that it would be necessary to re-arrange her friend's packing.

At last, after a week's preparation, the furniture was sold. It was more than enough to pay for their journey. M. Bienfait calculated that after arriving at Escaladios he would have a hundred francs left to buy the most necessary articles. They were to start the next day. All was ready,

Chapter XXXVI

Monsieur Jean Paul wished it

THE journey was a long pleasure for our two children, and even for their parents. Mme. Bienfait had never been beyond the walls of Paris. They were amused and enchanted with everything. "We are making the tour of France, as the nobility do," said they; —and yet the wooden benches on which they sat in the third class cars were very hard. Happy they who are contented, and amuse themselves everywhere!

Our good ladies the mice were of the party. Jean Paul was sure that they would be enchanted to return to their own country, and that the mountain air would bring back all their strength.

"Ah! then," said M. Bienfait laughing, "the air for the mice, the waters for my wife and me. We shall all be cured."

The little party entered triumphantly into Escaladios.

Chapter XXXVII

The good God permitted it

THERE is a large linden tree full of flowers before the forge. It was under its shade that the horses waited, as well as those who brought them.

The garden was fragrant with roses, with jasmines, pinks and sweet peas, and was quite inundated with sunshine. The interior of the forge was as dark as night; one could only see there the bright fire incessantly kept alive by large bellows; and a bar of red iron which two men struck, and kept time with the blows while singing. Then they sung no more, but they still struck on.

The song then commenced in the distance, the forge hammers accompanying it—Pan, pan, pan, pan!

It is at his mother's they are singing.

It is Madeleine and his sisters who answer Jean Paul and M. Bienfait.

Thus the days pass: they work, and they sing; they sing, and they work.

Jean Paul, however, passed a month quite alone the preceding year; his mother and sisters, Madeleine and Mme. Bienfait went to Bigorre to work there during the bathing season, and M. Bienfait followed them there.

274

The latter had worked there for a month as a lock-smith in the town. Every morning he took the famous baths, and drank the famous waters. Mme. Bienfait followed the same treatment.

When they both returned to Escaladios, Jean Paul found them looking ten years younger. Mme. Bienfait no longer suffered from that painful cough, nor M. Bienfait with the rheumatism.

What famous blows he could give with the hammer now! They came to his forge from all parts of the country. There was not a handsome horse that was not shod by our friend, and not a new house built that they were not employed to do the iron work.

And how well they sewed at his mother's! There was not a farmer's wife in the country who had not her dresses made by her daughters, particularly by the eldest, as they called Madeleine.

Mme. Bienfait and Jean Paul's mother took care of the two houses, the little gardens, the two cows, and they had also leisure time to rest themselves, and they were grateful to God for all His goodness to them.

My lady and Rosette lived on their income, in a fine large wire cage, hung from the ceiling of the forge. Our friends would not have a cat in the house.

www.ingramcontent.com/pod-product-compliance
Lightning Source LLC
Chambersburg PA
CBHW030957260626
47169CB00002B/587